BULLETS CAN'T STOP 'EM!

Marshal Josh Wade was standing at the barricade when one of the men in the posse heard the sounds first.

"Listen, what is that? Thunder?" the man asked.

"I don't see how it could be," Josh replied, looking up. "There isn't a cloud in the sky."

Everyone listened intently as the distant rumble grew louder.

"Look!" someone shouted, pointing to the west. "A cloud of dust! I've never seen such a dust storm!"

"Stampede!" the man standing on the roof of the livery yelled, cupping his hands around his mouth. "Stampede! They're coming right for the town!"

"Sonofabitch!" Josh roared. "Those damn-fool cowboys have stampeded their cattle! They're tryin' to kill us!"

The marshal stood mesmerized, watching the herd come nearer and nearer. Although he had faced down many a gunman, he was suddenly petrified with fear and unable to move. The ground was literally trembling with the thunder of four thousand hooves. Josh Wade, the sweat pouring down his face and soaking his shirt collar, was rooted with horror as the herd fast closed the distance between themselves and him.

The marshal could practically feel the hot breath of the animals on his back, and he was sure he and the others would be run down. Their movement seemed agonizingly slow, and it was as if he were in a nightmare . . .

Other books in the Faraday series:

IRON HORSE
COLLISION COURSE
THE GOLD TRAIN
THE COLORADO SPECIAL

FARADAY

THE TRACKWALKER
William Grant

Created by the producers of **Wagons West, Stagecoach, Badge,** and **White Indian.**

Book Creations Inc., Canaan, NY · Lyle Kenyon Engel, Founder

LYNX BOOKS
New York

THE TRACKWALKER

ISBN: 1-55802-185-X

First Printing/March 1989

Produced by Book Creations, Inc.
Founder: Lyle Kenyon Engel

This is a work of fiction. Names, characters, places, and incidents are either the product of the author's imagination or are used fictitiously. Any resemblance to actual events, locales, or persons, living or dead, is entirely coincidental.

Copyright © 1989 by Book Creations, Inc.
All rights reserved. No part of this book may be reproduced or transmitted in any form or by any means electronic or mechanical, including by photocopying, by recording, or by any information storage and retrieval system, without the express written permission of the Publisher, except where permitted by law. For information, contact Lynx Communications, Inc.

This book is published by Lynx Books, a division of Lynx Communications, Inc., 41 Madison Avenue, New York, New York, 10010. The name "Lynx" together with the logotype consisting of a stylized head of a lynx is a trademark of Lynx Communications, Inc.

Printed in the United States of America

0 9 8 7 6 5 4 3 2 1

FARADAY
THE TRACKWALKER

Prologue

HEADING TOWARD THE BRILLIANT SCARLET AND GOLD sunset beneath the darkening vaulted sky, the *Rocky Mountain Limited* raced across the flat Wyoming landscape. Inside the Baldwin 4-4-0 locomotive, the engineer held the throttle wide open while his fireman threw chunks of wood into the roaring flames of the firebox. The train was exactly on schedule, roaring past a milepost every one hundred twenty seconds.

Behind the engine and the tender was a string of coach cars, and, inside these, the passengers were getting down to the business of eating their supper. The cars that were for the most part occupied by immigrants seeking better opportunities out West than they had found in the East were filled with the exotic smells of smoked sausages, strong cheeses, and fermented cabbage. The day-coach passengers traveling from one city or town to another began opening the boxed meals they had bought for twenty-five cents at the previous stop. Or, if they were more affluent, they sat in the dining car at linen-covered tables set with gleaming china and sparkling silverware, ordering from expansive menus that could compete with the finest restaurants in the country.

Just forward of the dining car was the baggage car, where two men were waiting for their meal to be brought to them. One of the men was busy sorting mail; the other sat on a high, three-legged stool, holding a shotgun across his lap.

"What's taking Pat so long with our supper?" the man with the shotgun asked, pulling on his thick, dark beard. "I'm near to starving to death."

The towheaded young mail clerk chuckled. "If I know Pat, he's probably in the kitchen havin' a cup of coffee with the cook."

"Maybe you ought to go remind him we're waiting, Dabney," the guard suggested.

"Don't worry, Mr. Foster, he knows." There was a knock on the rear door of the car, and the clerk looked toward it. "Ah, there he is now."

"It's about time."

Martin Dabney laid his bundle of letters down and walked back to the door that opened onto the vestibule, unlocking it. "What took you so long, Pat?" he asked through the partially opened door. "Our detective friend was beginning to get—"

His words were cut off as the door was forced the rest of the way open, and four masked intruders rushed into the car.

"Get down!" the detective shouted to the mail clerk as he jumped from the stool and began swinging his gun to bear on the intruders. But before he could fire, one of them shot first. Catching a bullet in the stomach, Cedric Foster was propelled into the wall of the car, then slid down to the floor, the unfired shotgun clattering beside him.

"Kick that scattergun out of the way!" the leader of the intruders shouted, and one of his men sent the shotgun sliding across the floor, out of reach.

"Keep an eye on him," the leader then ordered.

"Hell, he ain't goin' nowhere," one of the bandits sneered. "He's gutshot."

Glaring at the mail clerk, the leader growled, "You want the same?"

Martin Dabney, his hands up in the air, backed away from the intruders. "No, sir. I ain't gonna cause no trouble. Don't shoot me, mister."

"Good. You're playin' it smart—not like that one," the leader noted, gesturing toward the fallen detective with the barrel of his pistol. Then he pointed to a pile of canvas bags. "Which one of them bags is for the Rocky Mountain Trust Company?"

"I don't know."

The gunman cocked his pistol and pointed it at the clerk's head. "Then you better find out in a hurry."

"Yes, sir," Dabney agreed nervously. With shaking hands, he sorted through the bags until he found the one he was looking for, then held it up.

"Here it is," he told the gunman. "I found it."

"Hell!" one of the other robbers said disgustedly. "There can't be much money if he can hold up the sack like that."

"It's paper money," the leader explained to his cohort. "Fifteen hundred dollars' worth—all in five, ten, and twenty dollar bills. It don't weigh that much, but it'll spend just as good." He grabbed the sack from the clerk, then pulled out his watch and looked at it. Nodding toward the door, he ordered, "Get it open."

A couple of the other bandits did his bidding, and the inside of the car was suddenly filled with the roar of wind and the sound of steel rolling on steel. The four intruders then all gathered near the open door.

"Now?" one of the men shouted to his leader, poised at the edge of the car.

"No, wait!" the leader said, examining his watch. He held his hand up; then, after a pause of about thirty more seconds, he brought it down sharply. "Now!" he shouted.

First the bag was tossed through the open door, and then the four men leapt out into the black abyss.

The clerk, still in a state of shock, held his hands up for a few seconds longer. Suddenly realizing that there was no longer anyone holding a gun on him, he hurried over to check on the wounded guard.

"Mr. Foster! Mr. Foster, are you all right?"

"Look out through the door," the detective gasped, his words slightly indistinct. "See if you can find out where they went."

Martin Dabney ran to the door and stared back into the darkness, but all he could see were golden squares of light projected from the windows of the passenger cars, sliding rapidly over the ground.

"I can't see a thing," he shouted.

"What time is it?"

"What?"

Cedric Foster coughed. "The time, boy. What time is it?"

It seemed like a strange request from a man so badly injured, but the young clerk pulled out his pocket watch and checked it. "It's exactly twelve minutes past seven o'clock," he announced.

"Remember that. It'll be important." Foster coughed again, and this time he coughed up blood. He tried to get up, shuddered, then fell back down. With one last rattle in his throat, he quit breathing.

Suddenly the door at the end of the baggage car opened again, and Pat, the other mail clerk, stepped into the car. Blood glistened on his forehead and ran down into his eyes from a wound on the top of his head. "What happened in here?" he asked, looking across at the detective slumped on the floor.

"We got robbed again! I guess they put you out of commission, huh?"

Touching his forehead gingerly, Pat answered, "Yeah. There was someone waiting for me when I came back from the dining car with your food. I got hit over the head and just now came to." Staring across the car at Foster, he asked solemnly, "What about the Faraday agent?"

"He's dead. They shot him right off," Martin Dabney breathed.

Pat pushed a shock of red hair out of his eyes as he observed, "This makes it four robberies in two months. If these bastards don't get stopped pretty soon, there ain't gonna be nobody trustin' the Union Pacific anymore."

"Hell, who's gonna stop 'em? The law? They haven't done a thing yet."

Shaking his head slowly, he advised, "This time's different. Cedric Foster was a Faraday man. When a Faraday man gets killed, Matthew Faraday doesn't stop till he finds out who did it. He'll be comin' after these fellas, you can count on that."

After hitting the ground painfully, rolling across gravel and sagebrush as the train roared on by above them, the robbers regained their feet one by one. Pulling off the bandanna that covered the bottom half of his face, the leader then climbed back up onto the track, brushing himself off as he watched the red and green lanterns of the last car grow smaller and smaller. Within a few more moments the ever-diminishing clacking of the steel wheels hitting the rail joints ceased, replaced by the soft sigh of the wind and the howl of a distant coyote.

"Everybody all right?"

"Seems to me like we could've found a softer place to land," one of the others grumbled.

"Yeah, I'm gonna be limpin' around for a week," another added.

"If you want horses to ride, this is where we had to jump," the leader informed them.

"Where *are* the horses?"

Gesturing, the leader said, "They'll be right up this draw." He threw the money sack over his shoulder, and he and the other three men started up a long, narrow gully. After about a half-mile walk, they saw four saddled horses standing quietly where they had been tied to several saplings.

"How'd they get here?"

"Our partner brought 'em."

"Is he around?"

"Nope."

"When we gonna meet him?"

"You don't need to meet him. *I* know who he is; that's enough."

"He ain't been gone so long. His fire's still smolderin'."

Ignoring the remark, the leader commanded, "Let's go. We got a long ways to ride before it gets light."

Chapter 1

JARED MACALESTER HAD BEEN VARIOUSLY DESCRIBED AS being all muscle and sinew and as tough and stringy as whipcord. The tall, handsome thirty-nine-year-old was all those things—but right now he was also bone tired, having walked the last five miles across the Wyoming plains hauling his saddlebags and tack. Finally reaching the raised trackbed of the Union Pacific line, he sighed wearily and then hefted his gear higher on his shoulders. He slowly climbed the ballast-covered slope to the top, the broken stones crunching loudly underfoot, where he thankfully dropped his gear alongside the tracks and scratched his week-old beard. Rotating his shoulders, he worked out the stiffness for a few minutes, then stepped onto the rails, looking eastward, his pale-blue eyes squinting into the distance. Stretched out before him as far as he could see was a twin set of tracks, connected by cross-ties that grew ever closer together as they were foreshortened by distance. Gradually the ties and rails disappeared on a horizon that was a sea of grass, unbroken by hill, tree, or bush.

He glanced at the sun, then tugged on his reddish-brown mustache that was just beginning to be shot through with silver. "Unless I've lost the ability to reckon time by the sun, a train should be along here soon." Then, having spoken the words aloud, he felt sheepish—for there was no one to hear them. Jared Macalester was not in the habit of talking to himself, though during the long and lonely days on the trail he often talked to his horse. Rationally, he knew that talking to a dumb animal was little more than talking to himself—but he reasoned there was just enough of a difference to make the habit acceptable in his eyes. But now even that excuse was gone, for he had lost his horse a few hours earlier when the animal had stepped into a prairie dog hole and broken his leg, necessitating shooting him.

Jared dropped to his knees and placed an ear to one of the iron ribbons, then smiled. He could hear a faint humming, and the vibration told him that an approaching train was just over the curve of the horizon.

Reaching into his saddlebag, he pulled out a yellow and red flag, a private signal that the Union Pacific had provided for him. The flag informed the engineer that Jared Macalester was a trackwalker, a man who rode or walked the tracks on the long stretches between depots, checking to make certain there were no damaged or obstructed rails.

Trackwalkers had several ways to signal engineers. A red flag meant danger, and it would inform the engineer to stop at once. At night or in foul weather, trackwalkers could place torpedoes on the track. When run over by the train, these gunpowder-filled cartridges would explode loudly enough for the engine crew to hear them, letting the engineer know that he should halt immediately.

A yellow and red flag, of the kind Jared was displaying now, called for the engineer to slow and proceed with great caution or to watch for someone on the trackbed and stop for a message. In this case, it was the latter reason—and Jared's message was that he needed a ride.

Squatting down and sitting on his saddle, Jared Macalester patiently waited, and the train appeared a few minutes later. It was approaching at a speed of better than thirty miles per hour, though the terrain was so open that it made the train's progress seem quite langorous. Against the vaulting sky the silhouette of the train seemed tiny, and even the smoke that poured from its diamond-shaped smokestack made little impression upon the vast panorama.

Jared could hear the train quite clearly now, the chugging of its engine carried to him across the wide, flat plain the way sound travels across water. He got to his feet and began waving the yellow and red flag, and he could tell almost immediately that the engineer had spotted him, for he heard the steam valve close, and the train began braking. Coming alongside him, the engine ground to a reluctant halt, puffing black smoke and wreathing itself in tendrils of white steam.

Two faces appeared in the window of the engine cab, both round, red, and decidedly Irish. One face was adorned with a large walrus mustache, and its owner—a man Jared judged to be nearing sixty—peered down at him.

"Well, now, my bucko, you'd be the new trackwalker, would you?"

"Yes, I am. Just started this section last week," Jared answered.

"Aye, and I told Donovan here—he's me fireman—the same. O'Brien's the name, an' I been runnin' this stretch of the road for the better part of a year now. But tell me, lad, what are you doin' out here afoot?"

"My horse stepped in a prairie dog hole," Jared explained.

"Aye, an' so it was necessary to destroy the poor beast," O'Brien sighed, shaking his head. "'Tis a shame, an' 'tis plain that you can't very well carry your supplies as you walk. Well, anyone who keeps the tracks clear is welcome aboard the train of Kevin O'Brien."

"Thanks. I'll just hurry on back to a coach," Jared told the engineer, gesturing toward the passenger cars. "That is, if you don't mind."

"Mind? Who could mind a trackwalker hitchin' a ride? Don't be daft, man," O'Brien assured him.

With another weary sigh, Jared picked up his gear and walked back along the tracks. Reaching the first car behind the coal tender, he climbed the steps onto the vestibule.

"Hey you!" The voice was loud, unpleasant, and challenging.

Jared turned around and saw a blond, blue-eyed man staring at him, his fists poised on his hips. Dressed all in black, except for the silver conchos on his belt and hatband, the young man looked as though he were itching for a fight.

"What the hell's going on? Are you the reason for this delay?" he demanded.

Nodding, Jared confessed in an easy tone, "I'm afraid I am. You see, I'm a trackwalker, and I needed a ride."

"Well, I'm a paying customer," the man said gruffly, "and I have a right to be delivered to Ironsprings on time."

The man's belligerence did not sit well with Jared. "Look, fella," he countered, "a trackwalker for the Union Pacific has the right to stop trains anytime he wants. Now, I'm not sure what you're so all-fired heated up about, because adding five minutes to this trip doesn't really make much of a difference, does it? So why don't you just return to your seat and quit worrying so damn much."

The man gave Jared one last angry glare, then spun around and stormed back inside the passenger car.

Shaking his head, Jared watched the young man's passage down the aisle of the car. He then stepped through the open door himself and dropped his saddlebags and tack in the front corner of the car, just inside the entry. The train started up, lurching slightly as it did so, and Jared waited for the motion to steady, holding on to the door handle, before maneuvering the length of the aisle.

As he waited, he studied the faces of his fellow passengers. He presumed that most of them were day trippers, local men and women who were making a short run between two close towns. But some were obviously long-distance travelers, and many of these appeared to be people who had chosen to emmigrate to the West. He idly wondered how many of the would-be farmers and ranchers had been drawn to these parts by the promise of a new life widely advertised by the railroads themselves.

Jared knew that it was very much to the Union Pacific's interest to attract as many people as possible to these wide open spaces. The railroad made money from the homesteaders by first selling them passage and then selling them farm land—for the railroads had been given vast tracts of land by the government to help finance the building of the rail lines. Once the land was settled, the railroads stood to make much more money for years to come from the day-to-day commerce, shipping produce and cattle from the farms and ranches in the West to the hungry markets in the East. To accomplish their end, the railroad spared no expense in advertising their land, taking full-page ads in newspapers and periodicals.

The movement of the train smoothed out, and Jared started up the aisle toward an empty seat half way through the car. Just ahead of it sat the young cowboy who had protested the stopping of the train, but he was staring sullenly out the window and did not bother to look up. As Jared gratefully sank into the seat, he glanced across the aisle and noticed a newspaper lying on the empty seat. A very pretty woman with copper-colored hair whom he guessed to be in her mid-thirties was sitting in the adjacent window seat, and when Jared nodded at her, she looked over and smiled, her brown eyes warm and friendly, and nodded back.

"Pardon me, ma'am, do you happen to know if the owner of this newspaper is through with it?"

The woman's smile broadened. "It's my newspaper, and you're quite welcome to it."

"Thank you very much," Jared replied, touching the brim of his hat and reaching across for the publication.

Settling back into his seat, he began reading the latest news, as reported by the *Ironsprings Vindicator*. This paper was much like many other newspapers in the West—heavy on the hometown news with a smattering of news from the outside world thrown in for good measure. Prominently displayed on the front page of this edition was an editorial that left no doubt as to the editor's point of view:

INCORPORATION NEEDED NOW

The recent imposition of a very stiff head tax on all cattle shipped from Ironsprings can only have a deleterious effect upon the future growth and well-being of our community. The ranchers will rightfully resent it, they will most certainly not pay it, and they will either drive their herds to a more forward-thinking community and load their cows there . . . or they will attempt to force the issue here, perhaps resulting in violence and bloodshed.

This would not happen if Ironsprings were incorporated.

The head tax was imposed by the Administration Committee, and while this newspaper recognizes that some source of revenue is necessary to run the town, we suggest that a better system would be a tax, equally applied, upon all our citizens. Of course, such a tax can only be assessed by a duly elected city council, serving an incorporated community whose charter is recognized by the territorial government of Wyoming. Perhaps the idea of a personal tax is not a popular one, but it is an idea commensurate with justice as well as the growth and development of Ironsprings.

The time for incorporation is now.

Jared read the entire paper, then folded it and put it aside. Yawning, he slouched down and propped his bent knees against the back of the seat in front of him. Then he tipped his hat down over his forehead, crossed his arms, and closed his eyes. He knew it would take but moments for his exhausted body to be lulled to sleep by the steady rocking motion and hypnotic clackety-clack of the wheels. But after all, there was plenty of time for a long nap before the train reached his destination—which happened to be Ironsprings.

Charlotte Baker had surreptitiously glanced at the man across the aisle as he read the editorial, trying to gauge by his expression what his reaction was. Her interest was not because she found him handsome—which she did—but because she was both editor and publisher of the *Vindicator*, having inherited the paper, the Washington Hand Press, and the drawers of type from her late husband. For almost twenty years, first in one town and then another, Cap Baker had published his newspapers, speaking his mind and defending the rights of the people. Charlotte, who was but seventeen when she married Cap, was by his side for fourteen of those years. She had been with him when their office was burned and the printing type destroyed by a band of ruffians in Kansas who disagreed with his politics. In Missouri, after a gang of night riders tarred and feathered Cap, Charlotte cleaned him up, then went back to the newspaper office with him to help him put out a special edition, naming his attackers.

When Cap died of apoplexy three years ago, Charlotte buried him in the desolate little cemetery just outside Ironsprings, then went right back to the office to keep the *Vindicator* going. Now, the paper was involved in as big a fight as it had ever faced, only this time the battle was being fought on the economic front. Charlotte was an avid and vocal supporter of incorporating the town, and many of her staunchest adversaries were also those whose advertising revenue she depended on. Despite their economic boycott, however, she continued the fight.

At least the railroad was supporting her. They had been placing two full-page ads a month in the *Vindicator*, and as a result of her visit to the regional headquarters in Cheyenne, that would now be increasing to four ads per month—one for every edition.

Charlotte loved newspapers—not just the business and editorial aspects, but the aesthetics as well. To her eyes, there was something beautiful about the printed page: the ink, shining so black; the paper, so crisp and white; the delineation between the two so sharp—nothing could be more striking.

Some people thought the newspaper business was not a fitting vocation for a woman. She smiled, remembering how after Cap died, a committee of well-meaning women called on her and offered to help set her up in a pie-making business until she could find another man to take care of her. They had been shocked when she told them that while she appreciated their help, she fully intended to continue putting out the paper—and, furthermore, she did not need a man to insure her well being.

But she had taken on part-time help. Not being able to afford to pay very much, she decided to look for a boy who would be interested in learning the profession and would be willing to start from the ground up—literally: sweeping the floors, cleaning the type fonts, delivering the newspapers to various locations, and assorted odd jobs. To her surprise, a then twenty-year-old youth named Johnny Rogers applied for the job. She had wondered why someone his age would not want a more substantial job than merely being a combination janitor-delivery boy, but Johnny seemed content. His satisfaction was even more bewildering in light of the fact that he had proved himself quite capable of working as a printer, for he had on occasion helped her with typesetting and pulling the sheets. But when she offered to promote him to a permanent position as printer—which would mean more responsibility and longer hours—he thanked her and politely declined, telling her he was not ready to "settle down" as yet.

Sometimes, despite her determination not to worry about him, her maternal instincts came to the fore— as when she saw him frequently of late hanging around the saloons or the Pleasure Palace, where the girls provided the services that lived up to its name. It was then that she wanted to tell him he could do better things with his time—and his hard-earned pay. In fact, she theorized that he must be stinting on his more basic needs in order to have any money left over to squander on such base pleasures. But she recognized that Johnny was now certainly old enough to know his own mind and his own needs, so she passed no judgment and they got along splendidly.

Even as Charlotte Baker was thinking about him, Johnny Rogers was delivering the latest edition of the *Vindicator*—which he had printed himself, setting the stories that Charlotte had written before she left—to all the paper drops in Ironsprings. Systematically making his rounds, he replaced the previous edition with the current one and collected the money that had been left, via the honor system. His final drop was the Bucket of Blood saloon, a false-fronted building at the westernmost end of the street that had a reputation as the toughest barroom in town. Here the liquor was cheap and green, often flavored with chewing tobacco and rusty nails. As a result, it dealt with a rougher clientele—men who were quicker to fight with fists or guns there than they were anywhere else but who were tolerated because they never complained about the rotgut they were swallowing.

As the young man switched newspapers, removing the two newspapers left from the last edition and leaving off a pile of the newer, one of the patrons called out, "Hey, Johnny! What kinda fire an' brimstone is the lady editor puttin' out today?" The man then strode over and reached out to pick up a copy.

"That'll cost you a penny," Johnny reminded him.

"Hell, no, it won't cost me nothin'." The man grinned broadly. "See, I'm one of them hardcases the newspaper's always writin' about—and if it wasn't for people like me, why, your boss lady wouldn't have nothin' to say. Then she wouldn't have no paper, and you wouldn't have no job." He grinned again, his expression more salacious. "And if you didn't have no job, Johnny, you wouldn't have no money . . . and them girls over at the Pleasure Palace wouldn't think you're such a fine fellow anymore. So, I reckon I'll just take this here paper for nothin'."

"No, I reckon you won't," a new voice, cold and clear, declared.

"Billy!" the would-be newspaper thief exclaimed, his face filled with both surprise and apprehension. Holding up the newspaper, he insisted lightly, "I'm just havin' a little fun with Johnny, that's all."

Billy Wade was the youngest of the three Wades who constituted the law in Ironsprings. He and his brother Adam were both deputies for big brother Josh.

"Pay for the paper, Tucker," Billy ordered.

"Sure, Billy, sure. You're the law," Tucker said.

Billy, the badge glinting on his vest, stood in the doorway and watched until the ruffian had returned to the bar. "I'm surprised to see you fellas without Tim Quick," he remarked to Tucker and his two cronies—who, like their friend, had always been referred to by their surnames; in fact, many people suspected that they did not even have given names. A sly smile on his face, Billy added, "You four are usually so close, I'm beginning to think that maybe you're really quadruplets."

The three men laughed, although it was clear that they had no real idea what they were laughing about.

Everyone in the bar waited to see if Billy would finally arrest one or all of them—although not even a minor infraction such as disturbing the peace had been committed. As Josh Wade often reminded any citizen who asked him, although Tim Quick and his cohorts were suspects in a number of robberies that had taken place outside Ironsprings, since the marshal's legal authority was confined to the unincorporated limits of town, he had no authorization to arrest them in his baliwick for any crimes committed elsewhere. Billy hated Ironspring's reputation as a haven for outlaws—although if a reward on a wanted man was big enough, brother Josh might well turn him in. It was rumored that as long as a man was willing to match—or preferably exceed—the bounty on his head, he could find sanctuary in Josh Wade's town. The marshal's view was best summed up in his favorite expression: "It's best we just take care of our own problems, and let the other folks handle theirs." Unless a flagrant illegality took place within their jurisdiction, virtually all the Wade brothers did was keep peace in the town—which in Josh's estimation was all that mattered.

As Johnny was about to leave the saloon, he stopped at the batwing doors and turned to Billy. "Thanks for your help, Deputy. Maybe we can have a drink together sometime."

Billy nodded perfunctorily. "Sure thing, Johnny."

The lantern hanging by the doorway threw eerie shadows into the yard as Ike, George, and Charley Stockard sat on the front porch of their rambling ranch house. The house was situated at the eastern edge of the fifteen-thousand acre spread that made up the Rocking S Ranch, and the roadway leading up to the yard was exactly five miles from Ironsprings' town limit.

Somewhere out in the darkness, a frightened calf bawled for its mother, and it was soon answered by a reassuring call. Ike Stockard, the oldest of the three brothers, smiled at the exchange, then leaned back in his chair and rolled a cigarette. He searched unsuccessfully in his pockets for a match, nodding his thanks when his brother George handed him one of his own.

"Ike, I hear tell cows is bringin' thirty dollars on the hoof back in Kansas City," George remarked. He whistled, continuing, "Boy, if we was to take a thousand head back to Kansas City, that'd be thirty thousand dollars! Whooee! Has anyone ever seen so much money?"

Ike did not respond but merely blew smoke rings that spiraled lazily upward, then dissipated in the night air.

"Ike, what do you think?" George persisted.

Shaking his head, the elder Stockard replied, "Sure, I'd like to take a thousand head to Kansas City. But how are we gonna get 'em there?"

"Why, we're just gonna take 'em into Ironsprings and put 'em on the cars," George replied.

"Just like that?"

"Sure. Why not just like that?"

"Maybe you don't know, but Josh Wade's put a head tax on all cows shipped out of Ironsprings."

"How much head tax?" George asked.

"The amount ain't important," Ike answered. "The thing is, Ironsprings ain't an incorporated town, and long as it ain't, nobody's got the right to charge any kinda tax at all. As far as I'm concerned, Josh Wade is no better than a cattle rustler if he's gonna charge us a tax to ship our own cattle."

"Seems to me if we want to drive our cows down to the depot and start puttin' 'em on the train, we've got enough hands to help us get the job done," Charley suggested.

"Not without bloodshed," Ike replied.

"I reckon that's true," Charley said. "But I figure we'll be sheddin' more of their blood than ours."

"Charley's right, Ike," George agreed. "There's not only our riders. Hell, if we wanted to fight this thing, we could probably get riders from all the ranches around here to throw in with us."

"I'm not all that anxious to get into a war," Ike said flatly, obviously wanting to close the subject.

"Maybe it won't come to that," Charley persisted. "Maybe if we just stand up and show the Wades we ain't gonna just set and be pushed around, they'll back off and leave us alone."

"Sure, and maybe if frogs had wings, they wouldn't bump their asses everytime they jump," George snorted. "Little brother, there ain't no way we're gonna get outta this without fightin'. So my thinkin' is why don't we just do it and be done with it?"

It was dark on the train now, the only light coming from the small lamps that burned dimly at the front and rear of the car. Jared Macalester had been dozing, and when the train started slowing down, the change in speed and rhythm awakened him.

The conductor entered the car from the rear, walking along slowly up the aisle. "Where are we, conductor?" one of the passengers asked.

"We're about ten minutes from Ironsprings, sir," he answered.

Those on the car who were going to detrain in Ironsprings started readying themselves. The ones who were continuing on settled back—some to spend a few more hours in their seats, others for another long and uncomfortable night of trying to sleep on the train.

Sitting up, Jared stretched his cramped body, then squared his hat and looked around. The young cowboy who had complained about the train stopping was not in the car. Neither was the attractive woman whose newspaper he had borrowed.

Deciding he needed to stretch his limbs and get some fresh air, Jared stepped out onto the vestibule at the front of the car—discovering that it was already occupied by the woman and the cowboy. He started to turn and step back inside to give them some privacy, but then he heard the woman's voice. It had an edge of fear that made him stop in his tracks.

"Please, Mr. Quick, I insist you leave me alone."

"Come on, a pretty widow-woman like you? You ain't foolin' no one. Once you get a taste of what it's like havin' a man around, you can't hardly go without one. I'm just offerin' my services, is all."

Jared's hand poised on the door handle when he heard the exchange, and he paused at the doorway and looked back at the two. He was reluctant to interfere in any discussion between a man and a woman because he knew that playing shy was often a woman's way. But this woman was not playing hard to get. She was actually frightened.

Turning around, Jared growled, "Sonny, it seems the lady doesn't want anything to do with you. Why don't you leave her alone?"

"What'd you say to me, old man?" the cowboy asked.

"I said leave the lady alone."

The cowboy's eyes narrowed as he studied Jared's face. "You're the trackwalker, ain't you? The man that stopped the train? Well, be advised, mister, that you already riled me once tonight. You obviously don't know me, or you wouldn't try to rile me a second time."

"Maybe you get riled too easily," Jared retorted.

Squaring his shoulders, the cowboy grated, "Yeah? And maybe I'm just gonna have to teach you a lesson. Permanent." He reached for his gun.

He got no further. Jared snatched the gun from the cowboy's hand before he could even get it raised, and then he grabbed him by the belt and collar.

"Hey! What are you—? Ahhhh!"

The cowboy's scream grew louder as Jared tossed

him from the train. He threw him far enough out so that the cars did not hit him—but he knew that the fall to the gravelly slope from even a slow-moving train had to be very painful.

"Sorry for the inconvenience, ma'am," Jared told the woman, his tone as light and casual as if he had just kicked a pebble from her path. He tipped his hat politely, then left her on the platform, staring at him in open-mouthed surprise as he stepped back into the car.

A few moments later she re-entered the car, making her way down the aisle and stopping beside Jared's seat. "Do you mind if I sit with you?" she asked.

"No. Not at all."

Sitting down, she arranged the mauve-colored skirt of her traveling suit, then told Jared, "I want to thank you for coming to my rescue."

He smiled and remarked, "I'm glad I could be of service."

"Did you enjoy the paper?" she asked, her gaze intense.

"Pardon?"

"The newspaper. Did you enjoy it?"

"Yes, thank you. Would you like it back?"

She shook her head. "No. I asked only as a matter of professional curiosity. You see, I'm Charlotte Baker, the owner and publisher of the *Ironsprings Vindicator*."

"Really? You don't see too many lady newspaper publishers."

"I suppose not," Charlotte replied, "but, you see, my husband got me into the business, and when he died, I decided to keep it going."

"I read the editorial about incorporation," Jared told her, scrutinizing her face. "I take it not everyone is for it?"

She sniffed in derision. "No."

"Why not? I would think that would be the goal of any town."

"Too many people are thinking about their pocketbooks," Charlotte explained, her anger evident in her voice. "The irony is that their thinking is so short-sighted, because in the long run an incorporated town would mean more prosperity for everyone."

Jared smiled, amused by her fervor.

"I'm sorry," she laughed. "I suppose I sound just like a politician, don't I?"

"Don't apologize. I think what you say makes sense. And I'm sure that your extremely persuasive editorials will soon convince those short-sighted citizens."

"I hope so—and thank you for the compliment." The train began slowing to a crawl, and Charlotte looked through the window—although by now it was too dark to see anything outside. "This is it," she announced.

"Beg your pardon?"

"Ironsprings. We're here."

Chapter 2

THERE WERE TWO PASSENGER TRAINS DAILY IN AND OUT OF Ironsprings. On the odd days, the trains were westbound; on the even days, eastbound. This being an odd day, the train approaching Ironsprings was headed westward. As soon as the train rattled to a stop in the station, Jared stepped down from the car and looked around. This was his first time in Ironsprings, but it was so much like a hundred other towns he had seen that he felt an immediate familiarity with the place. It was the kind of town that grew alongside the railroad, with each new business establishment claiming a rightful place anywhere it could find room. Rather than growing according to some master plan, Ironsprings was a loose collection of false-fronted buildings: a few saloons here, a bootmaker there, a hotel, a smithy, and a livery stable.

Jared pushed through the throng of people crowding the platform. This was the same wherever he went, too: Even though it was eight o'clock at night—an hour that found many people already in their beds—

there were dozens of townspeople gathered at the depot, for the arrival of the train—any train—was an event.

Making his way into the depot, Jared walked across the spacious room to the telegraph counter. He greeted the telegrapher and asked if he could temporarily store his tack and saddlebags in the baggage room.

"You a trackwalker?" the telegrapher asked, noticing the multi-colored flag with Jared's gear.

"Yeah," Jared confirmed. "I just started on this run, but I lost my horse in a prairie dog hole. I guess I can buy me a new mount here in town."

"That you can. Livery's down the other end of Front Street. Yeah, prairie dogs. You gotta watch them little critters." The telegrapher stuck out his hand. "Carl Masters is the name, Mister . . ."

"Macalester. Jared Macalester."

"Well, Mr. Macalester, you don't have to leave your tack in the baggage room. Bein' as you're an employee of the U.P., you can just bring it back here if you want."

"Thanks, Carl." Jared picked up his gear and carried it around behind the counter. As he was doing so, a well-dressed man in his fifties came in through the front door, greeting the telegrapher as he approached him.

"Carl, send a wire back to the Rocky Mountain Trust office in Cheyenne, will you? Tell them the money just arrived safely," the man announced, sounding both surprised and relieved.

Carl smiled and nodded. "It did, eh? Well, now, I reckon that's one that got away."

"Were you expecting the train to be robbed?" Jared asked.

The man noticed Jared for the first time and frowned. "Who are you?" he asked suspiciously.

"He's all right, Mr. Joyce. He's the new trackwalker. His name is Jared Macalester. This here is Ironsprings' banker, Rupert Joyce."

Jared smiled and extended his hand.

The banker hesitated for just a moment, then he took the offered hand. "I apologize for not being very friendly," he said. "I've learned to exercise caution around strangers. To answer your question, I don't know as I can say that I expected the train to be robbed, but I was worried about it. It's been robbed four times now, and I've lost two money shipments myself. The last robbery took the life of a Faraday man who had been hired to guard the money."

"Yes, I heard about that," Jared responded, nodding. "And they never caught who did it?"

Joyce shook his head in disgust. "I tried to get the marshal to go after the thieves as soon as the train arrived. I told him, 'Go now, while the trail's hot!' But Josh Wade didn't do a damned thing about it."

"Who's Josh Wade?"

"He's the marshal in Ironsprings, that's who," a gruff voice answered.

Jared turned toward the doorway. A man around forty with a lined, weathered face stepped into the depot. He stood in the entryway for a moment, hooking his thumbs into his belt, his shirt stretched across his slight paunch, then strode over to the banker. Pushing his hat back on his forehead, he scratched his graying sandy hair with his thumb. Then, his tone defensive, he said, "Be reasonable, Mr. Joyce. What exactly do you think my brothers and I can do? You know we don't have authority outside this town. Until someone decides to hold up a train while it's sittin' here in the station, there's not a damn thing we *can* do about these robberies."

The banker sighed. "I know, Marshal, I know. Well, maybe Charlotte Baker's right. Maybe we do need to petition the capital for incorporation." Taking the three men in with his glance, he declared, "Well, good night, Carl. Good night, Marshal. Pleasure meeting you, Mr. Macalester." With a pensive expression pinching his face, the banker left the depot through the same door he had entered.

"Did I hear my name mentioned?" a woman suddenly asked.

Jared turned at the familiar voice and smiled. "Hello again, Mrs. Baker."

"Charlotte, please," she insisted, stepping into the depot from the station platform.

Josh Wade walked over to Charlotte Baker and stood very close to her. "You two apparently know each other," he declared in a slightly petulant tone.

Ignoring the lawman's remark, Charlotte told Jared, "I want to thank you again, Mr. Macalester."

"Jared, please," he bantered, "and I'm glad I could be of service."

"What service?" Josh Wade interrupted, slipping his arm possessively around Charlotte's waist. "If you helped her out, maybe I owe you my thanks as well."

Charlotte deliberately slipped away from the marshal's arm. "For your information, Josh, Tim Quick was imposing himself upon me. And he was beyond annoying. I was beginning to get a little frightened of him."

"I see. And . . . Mr. Macalester is it?"

Nodding, Jared confirmed, "Yes, it is. Jared Macalester."

"And Mr. Jared Macalester had a few stern remarks for Quick, no doubt; informin' him that such behavior isn't gentlemanly." The marshal's words were taunting, almost caustic. It was obvious that he was a more than a little jealous of the fact that Jared Macalester looked good in Charlotte Baker's eyes.

"Not exactly," Charlotte said airily. She looked at Jared and smiled. "Mr. Macalester tossed him off the train."

"He did what?" Carl Masters interjected, grabbing the edge of his counter.

Charlotte turned to him, laughing. "He picked Mr. Quick up by the collar and belt, and tossed him bodily from the moving train."

The telegrapher shook his head slowly. "Mr.

Macalester, you're either the bravest man I ever met . . . or the most loco," he declared.

"Let's not make it into more than it was," Jared scoffed. "It was just some cowboy getting a little fresh, that's all."

"Tim Quick ain't no cowboy. He's more like what you'd call a gunslinger."

"A gunslinger, you say?" Jared stroked his stubbly chin for a moment, then he turned to Josh and smiled at him. "In that case, Marshal, I was about to have a drink. Maybe you'd like to join me. Might be good to have someone at my side for a while."

Josh Wade chuckled. "I'm no more anxious to run up against him than you." He broke into a broad smile. "But maybe if Charlotte would have a drink with us? . . ."

"Thank you, no," Charlotte responded. "Johnny— he's my assistant—is waiting to help carry the supplies I brought back with me over to the office. Then I'd better settle in for a few hours and catch up with things." She smiled warmly, adding, "As I said, I just wanted to thank you again."

For the first time, Jared noticed the young man— somewhat small in stature and bland of features and coloring—standing patiently in the doorway. Looking back at Charlotte Baker, he touched the brim of his hat and asked, "Some other time, perhaps?"

"Perhaps," Charlotte echoed. Bidding the men good night, she then turned and left the depot.

"Well, now, Mr. Jared Macalester," Josh began as soon as Charlotte Baker and Johnny Rogers had gone, "perhaps we'd better have that drink after all. If for no other reason than so's I can set you straight on a few things around here."

"Such as?"

"Such as who has claimin' rights on our lady publisher, and who doesn't."

"Seems to me like she's the only one who can assign those rights," Jared suggested.

"We'll talk about it," Josh promised earnestly, although there was a note of good humor in his voice. Steering Jared out of the depot, the marshal mused, "So, you tossed Quick out on his butt, huh?" He chuckled. "Yes, sir, I would purely love to have seen that."

As Jared Macalester and Josh Wade pushed their way through the batwing doors of the Bitter Drink Saloon, the piano player sitting at a shiny new upright against the back wall was tapping out a snappy version of "Buffalo Gals." A couple of women were sitting at a table nearest the piano, and from their dress and heavy makeup, Jared figured they were the very type the song was about. He smiled as he recalled something he had heard recently: The song was also popular back East, and it was often sung by very proper members of society. What they did not realize was that "Buffalo Gals" was simply another term for prostitute, so called by the Westerners because in the early days these women often spread buffalo robes on the ground on which to ply their trade.

The two men approached the bar and Josh slapped the gleaming countertop, calling to the bartender, "Sam, give my friend a drink on me."

Jared nodded and said, "Why, thanks, Marshal."

"Name it," the beefy bartender responded, setting aside the glasses he had been wiping with a cloth and grinning at the two new customers from underneath his dark walrus mustache.

"Whiskey," Jared replied.

"I'll have the same."

When Sam poured the drinks, Josh picked his up and held it toward Jared.

"Here's to you," he announced.

"Likewise. And thanks for the drink," Jared declared, returning the salute.

"And like I said, thanks for lookin' after Charlotte," Josh added. "You never know what kind of trouble a woman might run into, travelin' alone. After all—"

"Hey, Marshal, where's your brother Adam?" a voice filled with loathing suddenly yelled. "I got a score to settle with him."

Jared turned to see who had spoken, but Josh barely glanced in his direction. The man who called out was standing at the end of the bar, and when Jared looked his way, he took off his hat and pointed to a large knot on top of his head, clearly visible through his thinning, greasy black hair. He was exceptionally big—well over six feet tall and two hundred pounds.

"He liked to busted my skull when he conked my head with his pistol butt last night," the man continued, slurring his words drunkenly.

"As I recall, Bates, you were asked politely to leave the premises," Josh remarked nonchalantly, his eyes fixed on the bottles arrayed on a shelf behind the bar.

"Leave the premises? Ha! It weren't no premises. It was the damn Pleasure Palace—and I got a right to be in there, me as much as anybody."

"Not when you're drunk and abusin' the ladies."

"Ladies! They're whores!"

Shaking his head, Josh pointed out, "You're lucky it was Adam who came along and only whacked you on the head. If it'd been me, I might've shot you."

"Yeah? Well you tell your brother he better look out for me. I don't take havin' my skull busted without doin' somethin' about it."

"Bates, I think maybe you'd just better get on out of town," the marshal growled, his voice threatening.

"Why don't you just try an' run me out of town?" the man challenged.

Josh sighed quietly, then set his drink down and slowly turned toward Bates. The deliberateness of his movement caught everyone's attention as surely as if he had let out a shout. The piano player stopped in mid-chorus, and the saloon grew instantly silent.

"Bates, you don't really want to fight me, do you?"

Josh asked quietly, and in the silence his words filled the barroom.

At Josh's cold, calm words Bates's taunting attitude slipped visibly away. His face slackened and his eyes widened. Holding his hands out by his side, he said, "Now, wait a minute, Marshal. I ain't packin' a weapon. I want you to know that." He looked around at the others in the saloon. "I want all of you to know that. I ain't carryin' no gun, so if somethin' happens—"

"Is that how you're playin' it, Bates?" Josh cut in. "You start spoutin' off till you get called, then you back out 'cause you don't have a gun?"

"You ain't gonna shoot an unarmed man, are you, Marshal?"

"No," Josh replied, "I'm not goin' to shoot an unarmed man. But one of these times, I just may put a gun in your hand and *make* you fight."

Clearly reassured that Josh was not going to draw against him, Bates's confidence returned, and he smiled again, suggesting, "'Course, there's always fists. If you'd like to lay that gun on the bar . . ."

The bartender waved his arms. "Now, hold on, Bates. You goin' up against the marshal with fists is no more fair than him goin' up against you with guns. You got near fifty pounds and four inches on him."

"Yeah, I reckon I do at that," Bates agreed, smirking. "What about it, Marshal? You wanna try it?"

Josh poured himself another whiskey, then turned to Jared. "Like I was saying, Macalester," he blithely continued from where he had left off, completely ignoring Bates, "you never know when a woman travelin' alone might be accosted by someone who—"

"Marshal, look out!" Jared abruptly warned, for apparently emboldened by the fact that Josh was not going to draw against him, Bates had doubled up his fist to deliver a telling blow to the side of the lawman's head.

The warning was not needed. Even before Jared had

finished speaking, Josh had his pistol out of his holster. As fast as a striking snake, he first thrust the gun into Bates's face, then shoved the barrel into the man's mouth halfway down his throat and cocked it. The cylinder rotated just under Bates's nose, and he gasped, immediately lowering his fist.

"Bates, just what did you have in mind?" Josh asked coldly.

"Nothin'," Bates replied, the word jamming on the barrel of the Colt .44.

"I told you to get out of town," Josh reminded him, his voice steely. "That means now."

Eyes opened wide in terror, Bates backed away until the pistol-barrel was withdrawn from his mouth. There was a thin trickle of blood from where the front site had cut his lip, and he rubbed the wound with the back of his hand. "I'm goin'," he promised quietly. "Don't shoot! I'm goin'."

The marshal kept his pistol out until the man was gone. Almost before Bates exited through the swinging doors, the piano was again playing and conversation had resumed. Bottles clinked against glasses, and one of the "buffalo gals" shrieked with laughter over a ribald remark made by one of the patrons.

Holstering his gun, Josh Wade took a sip of his drink, then turned to Jared. "I want to apologize about that. Bates works for the Stockards—and to tell the truth, I don't understand how even the Stockards can put up with him.

"*Even* the Stockards?" Jared responded quizzically. "Just exactly who are they?"

Josh smiled. "Yeah, well, I suppose that sort of tells the story, don't it? They're ranchers, meanin' the Stockards and the Wades aren't exactly fast friends."

"I see. At least, I think I do. I read something about the head tax—which I presume is what all the fuss is about."

"I see you've done more than just be introduced to our lady publisher—you were introduced to some of her work, too." Lifting up his glass, Josh tossed down the rest of his drink, then announced, "Well, I've got to go. I'm still makin' my rounds."

"You go ahead, Marshal. And thanks for the drink—and the company." Jared shrugged, adding, "Maybe next time we meet, I can buy you a drink."

"I'll hold you to that," Josh said with an easy smile, then pivoted and crossed to the doors in two long strides. Jared watched the batwing doors swing to and fro for a few moments, then turned back to his drink.

An hour later, at the opposite end of town in the Bucket of Blood, Tim Quick stepped through the swinging doors and looked around the murky interior. Quick was a mess: His clothes were dirty and badly torn, there were scratches and bruises on his face, one of the silver conchos on his belt was missing, and the silver band around his hat was broken.

Tucker looked up from the table where he, Logan, and Grub were drinking, and his eyes narrowed at the sight of Quick. "What the hell happened to you?" he gasped.

Quick walked over to the table and sat down with his cohorts. Without a word, he reached for Grub's beer and took several swallows. Then, looking at the others with eyes flashing hate and anger, he growled, "I'm gonna kill the son of a bitch. I'm gonna kill him the moment I see him."

"Kill who?" Logan asked.

"The son of a bitch who threw me from the train, that's who!"

"You got throwed from the train?" Tucker asked, his eyes widening in amazement before he burst into laughter.

Quick had his pistol out in an instant. "You like that, do you?" he asked coldly.

"No," Tucker replied, his face sobering instantly. "No, Tim, I don't like that at all."

Shaking his head, a look of sympathy on his face, Logan asked, "Who did it?"

"I don't know the bastard's name, just that he's a

trackwalker." Quick put the gun back in his holster and Tucker breathed a sigh of relief.

"Tim, how'd that happen?" Tucker asked. "I mean, I can't see a fella doin' somethin' like that without you killin' him."

"The son of a bitch caught me by surprise," Quick rejoined. "I was standin' out on the platform between cars when he come up behind me. Next thing I know, I'm bouncin' and rollin' down the side of the track, and the train's goin' on without me."

"You was lucky you wasn't killed," Grub commented solemnly.

Quick snorted. "Yeah, well, the trackwalker ain't gonna be that lucky. Any of you see him? He's a big guy, with reddish-brown hair that's startin' to go gray, mustache, weathered face. . . ."

Laughter cut through Quick's words. He turned to see Johnny Rogers sitting at a table nearby, smiling gleefully. "You're not telling it the way I heard it," the young man said. "The way I heard it, you were bothering Mrs. Baker, and the trackwalker asked you to leave her alone. When you wouldn't, he tossed you off the train."

"Paperboy, what're you doin' in here drinkin' with men?" Tucker asked.

"Shut up, Tucker," Quick ordered. "I ain't interested in why he's here, I'm interested in the trackwalker." He stared at Johnny. "Do you know where this fella is now?"

Scratching his head, Johnny answered, "Well, I can't say as he's still there, but about an hour ago, he was goin' down to the Bitter Drink to have a drink with Josh Wade."

"Thanks," Quick barked. "Reckon I'll just go on down there myself."

"Tim, what if he's a friend of Wade's?" Tucker asked.

"Then I reckon Wade'll just have to find himself a new friend."

Tucker narrowed his eyes, cautioning, "You sure

about this? You know, angerin' Josh Wade? I mean, the way things is, long as we don't do nothin' against the law of Ironsprings, we got a place we can stay. Otherwise, we'd have to be on the run near all the time."

"Yeah," Grub agreed. "And if you just go in there and shoot that fella down, Wade's not likely to stand by and do nothin', if he's a friend."

Quick smiled. "Don't worry, it'll be a fair fight. I plan to push the old goat into drawin' on me."

"What if he won't do it?"

"Are you kiddin'? Believe me, this old coot has a temper. He won't stand there and let me call him everything but a man. Nope, he'll draw on me, all right—and when he does, I'm gonna put a bullet right in his gut."

"I'd like to come see that," Grub said, grinning.

"No, you'd better not," Quick responded. "If the marshal sees more'n one of us down there, he's liable to think we got it set up. You stay here." His voice dropped to a low murmur, and he added, "When I get back, I'll tell you about our next job."

Logan chuckled, asking, "You mean you got word from our— What do you call him?"

"Mastermind. Yeah, I got word from him. There's another shipment of money comin' through soon." Quick took another swallow of Grub's beer, then stood and hitched up his gun belt. "I had me 'bout a three mile walk into town, and I ain't used to walkin'. I'm gonna make that bastard pay for my discomfort," he announced.

"Tim?" Logan asked.

"Yeah?"

"What if . . ." Logan didn't complete the sentence.

"What if what?"

Logan looked as though he were sorry he had spoken. "This fella that threw you off the train, what if he's faster'n you?"

Quick's eyes narrowed and flashed angrily. "Logan,

are you tryin' to tell me I ain't fast enough to get the job done?"

"No, it ain't that. It's just—"

"It's just that you're a yellow-bellied coward and you think everyone else is, too," Quick offered.

"I ain't no coward!" Logan retorted hotly.

Tim Quick snorted, then mocked, "You ain't? You wanna draw against me?"

Tucker laughed nervously and stuck his hand out. "Easy, Tim. Logan didn't mean nothin' by it. He's just worried for you, is all. Besides, you wouldn't want to draw against one of your best friends, would you?"

Scowling, Quick reminded him, "I got no friends, let alone best friends. Just a few people I know, is all. And if I have to kill one of 'em, why, it ain't no skin off my nose. I'll just meet someone new. So anytime any of you boys want to try me, just let me know."

"No, no, we got no ideas about that," Logan assured him.

Quick pulled his mouth into what might have been a smile. "I'll take care of this little business right now, and then I'll give you the details on our more profitable business."

"Yeah," Tucker breathed, clearly relieved at the change of subject, "I'm ready for that."

Quick clamped down his black hat, then turned and strode across the saloon, pushing his way through the swinging doors with a determined expression on his face. Tucker, Logan, and Grub watched carefully until he was through the door, and as soon as he had disappeared from sight, Logan remarked, "That man is crazy. He's gonna get us killed."

"Wrong," Tucker said. "He's gonna get us rich. Then he's gonna get *himself* killed."

"Damn right," Grub laughed, finishing the one swallow of his beer that Quick had left him. "I like that. I like that a lot."

"Another drink, mister?" Sam asked.

"I'll have a beer," Jared Macalester answered.

"Then I need to find a good hotel, if you can recommend one."

"That's easy. The Cattlemen's Hotel, right across the street," the bartender told him.

"That's the best one?"

Sam laughed. "Hell, mister, it's the only one—unless you want to take a room over at the Pleasure Palace."

"The Pleasure Palace?"

"It's a whorehouse," Sam said. "But there's folks who have rooms over there."

"No, no, a real hotel will do," Jared laughed. "Wouldn't want anything to disturb my sleep."

Chuckling, the bartender turned to the beer barrel and pulled the handle, drawing a glass of beer, and Jared watched the man's movements. Suddenly, reflected in the mirror behind the bar, the batwing doors swung open and the cowboy Jared had thrown from the train—the man he now knew was Tim Quick—stepped inside. His face and clothes bespeaking the ordeal Jared had put him through, Quick stood by the door and looked around the saloon for a few moments. Then he stiffened when he spotted whom he had apparently been looking for: Jared Macalester. Jared forced himself to relax, loosening himself for what he knew was about to happen.

"You!" Quick shouted, pointing toward Jared. "The tall ugly old bastard standin' at the bar. Turn around, you son of a bitch, so I can watch your face when I kill you!"

Tim Quick's reputation as a gunfighter was obviously well known to the patrons in the saloon, for when they heard him yell, they opened up a path between Quick and Jared so wide and so fast that chairs, tables, cards, poker chips, and even drinks fell to the floor.

Slowly, Jared turned to face Quick. He let his hand hang casually by his side.

"You talking to me, Quick?" he asked.

"Yes. I'm talkin' to you, you son of a bitch! You sneaked up behind me and pushed me off the train!"

"No, I didn't sneak up behind you," Jared corrected, a wry smile playing on his lips. "I took you by the scruff of the neck and the seat of the pants, and I tossed you off like you were a mangy dog that was pissing on the floor."

At first, there was shocked silence from the others. They had evidently never heard anyone talk back to Tim Quick. Then a few people laughed, and others soon joined in. Within moments the whole saloon was laughing . . . and they were all laughing at Tim Quick.

"You bastard! You bastard!" Quick sputtered. "You've got them all laughin' at me! Pull your gun! Pull it, you son of a bitch, or I'll shoot you dead anyway!"

"Anytime you're ready, Quick," Jared told him.

Suddenly a figure stepped through the batwings, dashed up behind the cowboy, and brought the butt of his pistol down on Quick's head. When Quick fell to the floor, the man who had hit him holstered his gun and brushed his hands together as if he had just completed an odious task.

"You two," he directed the men who were the closest, "take him down to the jail and let him sleep it off."

"All right, Marshal," one of them answered.

"Hello, Josh," Jared said laconically. "I'm glad to see you came back."

"I had to. This is part of my rounds," Josh explained. He nodded his head toward Quick, who was now being dragged out of the saloon. "Looked like Quick was about to do you in." Suddenly the marshal's dark eyes narrowed, and he studied Jared carefully. "Unless you know somethin' I don't."

"Like what?"

"Like why you weren't afraid of him. Looked to me like you were about to stand up to him."

Jared smiled. "Well, now Josh, I'm a big boy. What

the hell was I supposed to do, wet my britches? Quick was about to throw down on me . . . and from where I stood, it didn't look like I had any choice."

Josh laughed heartily. "I guess you're right. Look, do you think you can stay out of trouble for the rest of the night? Like I said, I got rounds to do. I can't be spendin' all my time looking after you."

Jared returned the laugh. "Don't worry about me, Marshal. I'm headed for the hotel now. I've had enough excitement for one day."

Jared lay in bed in the second floor front room of the Cattlemen's Hotel. It was after midnight, but he could not sleep. Lying there, he listened to the sounds coming up from the street. Not only were the Bitter Drink and the Bucket of Blood still open and doing business, sounds of revelry were coming from the Pleasure Palace, as well. Jared knew the establishments would remain open until nearly dawn.

Putting the noises out of his mind, he thought about what had actually brought him to this town. He turned to the bedstand and lit the kerosene lamp, then picked up the folded letter he had read at least a dozen times, as if rereading it again would somehow provide clues.

Though Jared knew its author had one of the new typewriting machines, this letter was written in the neat, bold penmanship of Matthew Faraday's personal assistant:

June 20th, 1884

Dear Jared:

As you have been previously informed, our friend and fellow agent, Cedric Foster, was killed during the performance of his duty while guarding a money shipment on board a Union Pacific train. The robbery that cost Mr. Foster his life was the fourth that the railroad has recently endured.

Mr. Barth Cavanaugh, a vice president of the Union Pacific Railroad, has signed an agreement on behalf of the U.P. to engage the services of our agency to locate and arrest the train robbers. I need not tell you that the perpetrators of the robberies and the murderers of Mr. Foster are the same. Therefore, it will be of particular satisfaction to me to see this case solved.

The solving of this case is, in fact, your next assignment. To that end, I have arranged for you to assume the cover of a trackwalker while investigating this case. It is my belief that such a disguise will enable you to secure information that might otherwise be hidden from you, were anyone to know your actual vocation. Therefore, for the duration of this assignment, you are directed to tell no one of your association with this agency.

Always anxious to be of whatever service you might require, I remain,

Yours sincerely,
Matthew Faraday

Chapter 3

A GENTLE BREEZE FILLED THE WINDOW CURTAIN, CARRYING with it the aromas of a new day: bacon frying in a pan, fresh coffee, and the strong though not unpleasant smell of horseflesh warming in the early morning sun.

After rubbing his eyes, Jared Macalester stretched, then got out of bed and walked over to the window to look onto Front Street below. The town appeared as quiet this morning as it had been boisterous the night before. Merchants were already preparing for the day's commerce, and baskets of potatoes, onions, apples, and oranges displayed on the porches in front of the stores shared space with ax handles, grub hoes, and brooms. A few doors down the street, the butcher was dressing a side of beef while a dozen dogs waited expectantly for the scraps he was throwing them. A freight wagon lumbered slowly through the town, heading for the depot, where its contents would be off-loaded and stacked to await the next train east that, according to the clock on the wall, was due in a few hours.

"If it doesn't get stopped by train robbers before it gets here," Jared muttered under his breath.

He sighed heavily. Never had the Faraday agent started an investigation with fewer clues as to who the guilty parties might be. After the most recent robbery, he had read the mail clerk's statement and learned that the robbers had jumped from the train "exactly twelve minutes past seven o'clock."

The clerk had not understood why Cedric Foster had been so insistent upon establishing the time, but Jared knew. By computing the time and speed of the train, he had been able to establish distance. Then by using a route map provided by the Union Pacific with the mileage clearly marked, he easily located where the train had been at ten minutes past seven on the night of the robbery.

Following Matthew Faraday's instructions, under the guise of inspecting the track, Jared had ridden to that spot where—after a brief search—he located a canvas bag marked "Rocky Mountain Trust Co."

To one as experienced at reading signs as Jared Macalester was, the area where he found the sack told a relatively complete story of what had happened. He estimated that five horses had been there, as evidenced by the number of hoofprints and also by how much grass had been cropped by the horses as they waited. There were also the remains of a campfire and coffee grounds from a pot of coffee. The amount of grounds indicated that only a small portion of coffee had been brewed, probably no more than one or two cups. There were also two crushed-out butts and a piece of orange peel, indicating that whoever waited there had smoked a couple of roll-your-owns and eaten supper.

Jared had thought how ironic it was that the railroad itself made his job more difficult. There had been a time when finding an orange peel would have been lead enough to pinpoint the robber to a specific town, as oranges were once a fairly rare commodity on the plains. But with the coming of the railroads, oranges from California and Florida found their way all over the country and were now as staple a fare in grocers' barrels as apples or potatoes.

Assessing the area, Jared had decided that one man had waited here—one man, with five horses. When the four robbers completed their business on board the train, they timed their jump so their confederate would be waiting to meet them. He had to admit that it was a pretty slick operation.

The agent had easily found the trail where the men had ridden away, discovering that one of them had ridden off in a completely different direction from the other four. For a moment he had been puzzled as to which trail to follow, then he decided to follow the foursome. But in so doing, his horse stepped into a prairie dog hole, and Jared had no choice but to shoot the poor animal, then walk back to the tracks and wait for the next train. His destination was the only sure thing about this case, for it turned out that this latest crime, along with the three others in the recent string of robberies, had all taken place within a forty-mile radius of the town of Ironsprings. One other finger had pointed to this town as being the one where he would make his headquarters during the investigation: Lying near the campfire, he had found a copy of the *Ironsprings Vindicator,* dated the same day as the robbery.

Now, with a good night's sleep under his belt, he turned from the window, deciding he had more important things to do than contemplate the peaceful streets of Ironsprings. Crossing the room to the washstand, he poured water from the rose-colored porcelain pitcher into the matching basin, then quickly washed and shaved. His morning ablutions completed, he got dressed and left his room. Descending the stairs, he nodded to the desk clerk as he strode across the lobby and left the hotel.

Immediately next door was a restaurant, and having had relatively little to eat the day before, Jared was as hungry as a bear. He went inside and sat at a table by the window where he was almost instantly waited on by a plump, middle-aged woman who smelled of flour and spices. The aromas were pleasant to Jared, and for a moment he recalled his mother's kitchen back in Missouri when he was a boy.

"You look like a man who could enjoy a big breakfast," the woman observed.

Nodding enthusiastically, he rejoined, "Could enjoy it and will enjoy it." He smiled, then asked, "Do you have any suggestions as to what in your kitchen would satisfy a very hungry man?"

"Pork chops, eggs, biscuits and gravy, with a side of pancakes," she offered.

"Add a good-sized pot of coffee, and that should just about take care of me."

The woman smiled broadly. "Ah, good, good. I like a man with a big appetite. By the way, my name is Millie," she announced, then turned and headed for the kitchen.

Jared saw a new edition of the *Vindicator* lying on one of the vacant tables, and he read it while he waited for his breakfast. He had just finished it when Millie, balancing steaming plates climbing up both arms, brought his breakfast to him. She sat enough food before him to feed three men, but Jared made a brave resolve to eat as much of it as he could since he was certain the waitress had gone out of her way to be generous in the servings.

"That does look good," he told her as she put a plate of biscuits and a bowl of gravy before him.

"I thought you might like it," Millie declared, beaming. She gestured toward the paper. "I see you've been reading our local paper. Its nice, a little town like this having a newspaper of its own, don't you think?"

"Yes, I do. I met the publisher yesterday on the train. I have to confess, she doesn't look like any newspaper owner I've ever seen before."

Millie chuckled. "Don't let her gentle looks fool

you, mister. She's her own woman, and she don't mind taking on anybody."

"What does the rest of the town think about her?" Jared was not certain where he was going with this line of questioning, but since he had found a copy of the paper at the site where the train robbers had met, it was, so far, his only substantial clue.

"Mister, if you want to know what folks in this town is thinking about anything, you should go down to the depot around eleven o'clock."

"The depot?"

"Sure. Everybody goes down there to watch the trains come and go, and I guess it's become sort of a town meeting hall." She grinned, adding, "Whatever anybody has on their mind gets said down there, believe you me."

"Thanks," Jared laughed. "I just might do that." He looked down at the array of food in front of him and winced. "That is, if I'm still able to stand when I'm finished."

Millie's merry laughter trailed behind her all the way back to the kitchen.

Though he made a valiant effort, Jared was unable to put away the entire breakfast. He did a credible enough job, however, to win an approving smile from the waitress as he left.

For the rest of the morning, Jared wandered around the town. Once, when he was across the street from the newspaper office, he caught a glimpse of Charlotte Baker through the big plate glass window. He thought about going over to talk to her, but she seemed so busy that he knew he would just be in the way. He would see her later, perhaps, after she was finished with her work. Finally, at about a quarter to eleven, Jared found himself at the depot.

Just as Millie had said, the depot platform was full of people, and as she had also promised, there were several points of view being offered on everything from whether there would be a rain soon to the relative merits of mules over horses for farm work. There was a good deal of talk about the upcoming Fourth of July celebration, with some emphasis on whether or not Lefty Hughes, the pitcher for Ironsprings' baseball team, would have his "stuff" working well enough to take the measure of the Green River nine. There was also a lively discussion taking place among three male citizens about the editorial Jared had read in the *Vindicator*.

"I don't care what the editorial said, I'm tellin' you we're just as well off without bein' incorporated," one man declared.

"Yep, I'd just as soon stay the way we are," another put in.

A third man spoke up and pointed to the second speaker, "You, I can't understand. Him"—he pointed to the first speaker—"I can see. He owns the leather goods store and he's on the Administration Committee, so he's got some say in what goes on around here. You and me got none."

The shopkeeper retorted, "Maybe not, but what difference does it make? I mean, we got law and order, don't we?"

"We got only what law and order Marshal Wade can give us in town. But you know damned well that if you get on a stagecoach or on a train and go no more'n a mile out of Ironsprings, you got no protection at all. There ain't nothing the marshal can do for you."

Shrugging, the shopkeeper allowed, "All right, maybe it ain't the best, but it's good enough—and there ain't no taxes bein' charged the common folk. Only ones payin' taxes in this town are the businessmen."

"So, what you're saying is you're willing to sell your soul just to get out of paying some taxes?"

"What I'm sayin' is I got no complaint against things the way they is now."

"I wish you'd tell that to the newspaper editor," the Administration Committee member put in. "If she keeps up her bellyachin' in her paper, the territorial government's gonna come down here and force us to incorporate. When that happens, we're gonna have rules and regulations that'll kill off all our business. You mark my words." Clapping the shopkeeper's shoulder, he remarked, "I'm glad to see you're not advertisin' with her. Maybe if more of the merchants would stop usin' her, she'd go belly up."

"That ain't likely. She just paid off the buildin' she's in—and I know for a fact that it cost her near a thousand dollars, so I don't seem to be hurtin' her none."

Eventually the discussion got around to the ill will between the ranchers who lived outside of town and the people who lived in the town. Some hated the fact that the ranchers would let their hands come into Ironsprings where they'd drink and get rowdy and destructive—kicking in a few windows and breaking up some tables and chairs—and in general make themselves very unwelcome. Others believed putting up with them was a necessary evil, because the merchants in town depended on the ranchers and their hands for more than half of their business.

"It don't go only one way," one of the men insisted. "They need us as much as we need them."

Shaking his head firmly, another offered, "Yeah, but we don't go out to their places to have a good time. They like comin' in, but when it comes time to pay the piper, they don't want no part of it."

"You mean like the head tax on the cattle?"

"Yeah, the head tax. Seems to me like that's no more'n fair. After all, most of the work of the marshal and his deputies is in keepin' them from tearin' up the town in the first place. It only seems right that the ranchers should have to pay their share of the cost."

"You gotta admit, though, five dollars a head is a pretty steep tax."

"The marshal needs that money," one of the men said.

"Don't kid yourself. Josh Wade's got more money

than anyone in this town, what with the whorehouse and the saloons."

"I didn't say he wasn't a good businessman. But you don't expect him to use the money he makes from his personal businesses to run the town, do you? For that, he's going to need money from the ranchers. And since they don't live in town, they ain't too keen on the idea of payin' taxes."

"You think they'll come around?"

"Ike Stockard's the key," one of the men said. "The Rocking S is the biggest spread around these parts, and Ike's got all the other ranchers watchin' him. Whatever he does, the others will follow right behind."

One of the men laughed scornfully. "Makes you wonder, don't it? There ain't a man in Wyoming don't know the size of the loop Stockard used to throw."

"What do you mean?" one of the younger men asked.

Sneering, the man answered, "He threw a wide loop—meanin' he wasn't always sure whose brand was on the cows he roped."

"Some say he might've stopped a stage or two in his early days, too," one of the others put in.

"Yeah? Well, that's somethin' I wouldn't be goin' aroun' sayin' if I was you. Most ranchers don't mind bein' accused of throwin' a wide loop—hell, I reckon at one time or another, most all of 'em have done it—but holdin' up stages is somethin' else again. And a man with Ike's temper might not like hearin' that said about him."

The man who had made the suggestion in the first place cleared his throat nervously. "Well, uh, I didn't say he done it. I just said I . . . uh . . . heard that maybe—" His nervous explanation was interrupted by the whistle of the train.

Jared Macalester had overheard the entire conversation, and he found it very interesting. If it was true that Ike Stockard had held up a few stages in the past, it would not be that farfetched to suspect that the rancher had graduated to robbing trains.

While Jared Macalester was leaving the train depot and heading back toward the center of town, just down the street in the jail, Billy Wade, the youngest of the three Wade brothers, was turning a key in the door of Tim Quick's jail cell. Taller than Josh, with broader shoulders and a handsome, kindly face, there was nevertheless a similarity in their features and their coloring. The middle brother, Adam, who was sitting behind the desk, also bore a striking resemblance to his brothers. However, whereas Billy and Josh were clean shaven, Adam had a light-brown handlebar mustache, the ends of which were stained with chewing tobacco.

As Billy swung the cell door open, Quick growled, "It's about time you let me out of here."

"Just following Josh's orders. He said not to let you out too soon," Billy countered.

Quick, who had spent the time in jail mending the silver band around his hat, put the Stetson on his head and asked, "Where's my gun?"

"It's over there, hanging from the peg," Billy replied, pointing to the silver-decorated holster and gun belt.

The black-garbed cowboy grabbed the gun belt and buckled it on.

"Quick," Billy warned, "don't go looking for that trackwalker you braced last night."

Quick snorted. "Sorry, Deputy, I can't agree to that. Me and that feller's got some unfinished business to take care of."

"If you go up against him and live, then you're gonna have to go against Josh, too," Billy declared. "You know that, don't you?"

Sneering, Tim Quick taunted, "Think I'm afraid of your brother?"

"Josh might not even enter the picture," Adam

called out. Leaning back in his chair, he continued, "I just might take care of you myself. Can't say as I ever cared much for you anyway, Quick."

Quick laughed. "Josh is a hell of a lot faster'n you, and he don't scare me. You think I'm gonna worry about you?"

Adam smiled broadly, then worked a quid of tobacco so that he could spit it through a gap in his front teeth into the spittoon by the corner of the desk. "You don't understand how it works, do you, Quick? Fast ain't got nothin' to do with it. Hell, I ain't tryin' to build no reputation like you. I'll just sneak up behind you and let you have two barrels of double-aught buckshot right in the back of your skull. There won't be enough of your head left to hang that purty hat on."

Quick swallowed once, then forced himself to smile. "Maybe you ought to stop and think afore you go makin' that kind of threat. You know, you ain't the only one can do somethin' like that. But it don't matter none, anyway, 'cause I got more important things to do than waste my time goin' after a trackwalker."

"I thought you might see it that way," Billy chuckled.

Tim Quick stepped out onto the porch in front of the jail, with Billy following right behind him. Both of them spotted Jared Macalester walking toward the marshal's office from the direction of the depot.

"Goddamn!" Quick exclaimed angrily at the sight of the man who had thrown him from the train. "Goddamn!" he repeated. "I ought to—"

There was the ominous, metallic click of a pistol hammer being thumbed back and a cylinder revolving. Then Billy Wade shoved his pistol into the gunslinger's back. "Have you forgotten our little talk already, Quick?" he asked.

Tim Quick stood there with his face flushed, silently fuming, his frustration evident. Finally he turned and walked away from the jail. The young lawman watched him for a moment, then slipped his revolver back into his holster.

As Jared neared, the deputy smiled broadly and extended his hand. "You must be the trackwalker my brother told me about. I'm Billy Wade."

"Jared Macalester."

"Had lunch, Jared?"

Jared patted his stomach. "No, but I had a breakfast large enough to stuff a bear."

Billy laughed heartily. "You must've eaten in the Cattlemen's Café. Millie—the woman that works there—sure does believe in a big breakfast. Come on, I'll buy you a cup of coffee."

Jared walked with Billy toward a small restaurant a few doors down. The townspeople they passed on their way smiled and greeted the deputy, and even a ranch hand riding by in the street waved at him.

Reaching the restaurant, they went in and sat down, ordering coffee for Jared and a ham sandwich for Billy. As soon as the waitress walked away, Jared commented, "I didn't think I'd see that."

"See what?"

"A ranch hand waving at you. I thought there was a lot of hard feeling between the townfolk and the ranchers—and especially between the ranchers and you lawmen."

"Yeah," Billy allowed, "I guess there is. Seems foolish, though. Seems like we could work things out without letting it get this far."

"You mean the head tax?"

"Yeah. That's got all the ranchers pretty upset. I told Josh . . ." Billy stopped in midsentence.

"What? To drop it?"

"No, not exactly. Don't get me wrong, Jared, we need some way to raise revenue in this town. But five dollars a head seems pretty steep. I can't say as I blame the ranchers for being mad."

"What about the incorporation issue?" the agent asked. "I get the impression that Charlotte Baker leads the group that's for incorporation, and your brother Josh is the leader of the group that's against it."

"Your impression is correct," the young lawman confirmed as the waitress brought his sandwich to the table.

"What about you, Billy?" Jared questioned. "Where do you stand?"

Billy paused with the sandwich halfway to his mouth, and Jared could tell by the expression on his face that he had asked a question the deputy had often pondered.

"I wish I could tell you right out where I stand," he finally answered. "On the one hand, I think Charlotte Baker has some good points on her side. I don't think Ironsprings is going to survive much longer if we don't incorporate. On the other hand . . ." He paused, seeming almost reluctant to complete the thought.

"On the other hand?"

"My brother's against it," Billy said flatly, adding softly, "and he is my brother."

"That's it?"

"That's enough. I believe in loyalty to one's family, Jared."

The Faraday agent took a sip of his coffee and studied the young man over the rim of his cup. He liked Billy, and he empathized with his dilemma. One of these days Billy Wade was going to be forced to make a hard decision—and no matter which way he went, he was going to come out the loser.

Tim Quick had walked away from the jail and straight to the Bucket of Blood saloon. His three cohorts, as usual, were sharing a table there, and as soon as he walked in, Grub signaled the bartender, who delivered an extra beer to the foursome. Tucker pulled out a chair for Quick, and the gunslinger sat down heavily, grabbing the glass of beer and downing it in one long pull. Wiping his mouth with a satisfied sigh, Quick breathed, "That was good. Didn't have nothin' like that in that pigpen Josh Wade calls a jail."

"You should've let us go to the Bitter Drink with you," Tucker mused. "I heard how Josh come up behind you and hit you over the head like he done."

"Yeah," Grub noted, "we could've at least watched out for that."

"What I don't understand," Logan added, "was why the marshal decided to mix into it in the first place. What's the trackwalker to him, anyhow?"

"You forget Wade's been sniffin' around the lady publisher," Grub answered. "Maybe he was tryin' to show off for her."

Logan snorted, then quipped, "Well, seems to me like there's gonna be a showdown comin' soon twixt the Wades and the Stockards—and when that happens, I figure old Josh Wade's gonna want as many on his side as he can get. Hittin' folks on the head with his gun butt don't seem like the way to go about winnin' too many friends."

"Yeah," Tucker chuckled, "it's gonna be interestin' to see what Josh and Ike are gonna do when the shootin' starts between the Stockards and the Wades."

Grub swallowed a mouthful of beer, then declared, "To tell the truth, I'm kinda lookin' forward to seein' that. I figure it'll be a pretty good show."

"It'll be more than a good show," Quick finally put in, smiling with wicked amusement. "There's gonna be some pieces left layin' around to pick up—and we're gonna do just that."

"What do you mean?"

"If the Stockards win, then this town's gonna need a new marshal and deputies," the gunslinger pointed out.

"So?"

Quick's smile broadened. "So . . . how would you boys like to be my deputies?"

Grub laughed and polished an imaginary badge on his shirt. "Yeah, one of them tin stars would look pretty good here."

"What if the Wades win?" Logan asked.

"Then I know where there's gonna be some cattle we can pick up . . . real cheap," Quick noted.

The men laughed, then ordered another round.

It was late afternoon before Jared Macalester found his way into the Bitter Drink Saloon. As it was too early for the evening trade, the saloon was considerably more subdued than it had been the previous night. Now the piano was silent, an empty glass and full ashtray the only evidence that a man had been playing it for hours the night before, and the barroom sported very few patrons.

Two people sat at the table nearest the piano, a middle-aged cowboy Jared had heard called Dingus, and Katie, the lone bar girl working at this hour. The fact that each of them had only one glass before them indicated that Katie had accepted the slowness of the afternoon.

There was, however, a lively card game in progress. Five men ringed a table littered with poker chips and empty beer mugs. There were two brass spittoons within spitting distance of the players, but despite their presence, the floor was riddled with expectorated tobacco quids and chewed cigar butts.

Suddenly one of the players threw his cards on the table in disgust, then stood up. "I've had enough of this," he growled, wiping his sweaty palms on his dirty denim pants. Brushing a shock of brown hair out of his eyes, he demanded, "Hunter, how much longer we gonna stay around here?"

"What's your hurry, Pete?" a roughhewn man of about forty-five replied, a glint in his pale eyes.

"If you'd been gettin' hands like me all afternoon, you wouldn't ask that. I've lost fifty bucks."

Hunter reached into the pocket of his checked shirt and pulled out a small cigar. "So you lost some money, so what? We can always get some more."

Pete laughed gruffly at his friend's comment. "Yeah," he agreed, relaxing somewhat. "Yeah, I guess we can."

"You fellas got a gold mine somewhere or somethin'?" one of the other players asked. Jared recognized the speaker as the ranch hand named Bates. He seemed to have recovered from his run-in with Billy.

Both Hunter and Pete laughed, and then Hunter answered, "You might say that, eh, Pete?"

"Yeah, you might." Pete responded, looking over at the table where Katie was sitting with the cowboy. Gesturing at the woman, he asked Dingus, "Hey, you, you old coot. You gonna take that girl upstairs or just sit there and jawbone her to death?"

Dingus turned in his chair and looked at Pete, then shrugged. "You go ahead, sonny. Take her upstairs. I'll still be here when she's finished."

"Come on," Pete growled at the girl as he walked over and stood beside her. "Let's go."

"Couldn't you be a little friendlier about it?" Katie complained, looking up at him with disdain.

"I got the money; I don't need to be friendly," Pete countered. He then roughly took hold of her arm and pulled her to her feet.

"Easy, mister," Dingus put in. "That ain't no way to treat a woman."

"She ain't no woman," Pete sneered. "She's a whore. I ain't payin' her for the privilege of bein' nice to her. Come on, you," he repeated to Katie, propelling her toward the staircase. "Let's go."

With a long-suffering sigh, Katie started up the stairs with Pete.

From where he stood at the bar, Jared watched the scene with detachment. Although it would be easy to conclude that the bar girl was being mistreated, she clearly had had a great deal of experience in handling her clients and would only resent any intrusion. Mentally shrugging, Jared turned back to the bar and sipped his drink.

At that moment, the batwing doors swung open and Josh Wade stepped into the saloon. Turning at the sound of the swinging doors, Jared smiled when he saw it was Josh entering and started to greet him. But the marshal did not even seem to be aware of his presence, and then Jared noticed by the expression on his face that he was not paying a social call.

"John Hunter!" Josh shouted, flipping his coattail back over the handle of his pistol as he issued the call. There was a definite note of challenge in his voice, and the others in the saloon, obviously recognizing the danger, began to scatter out of the way. Even Jared moved down to the far end of the bar to be out of the path of any wild shot, should shooting occur.

Hunter stood up and looked across the room at Josh. There was a wry smile on Hunter's face.

"Well, well, well. If it ain't Josh Wade. Last time I seen you, Wade, you was back in Hays City. But you wasn't wearin' no badge then. Let's see, just what was it you was doin'? Oh, yeah, you was ridin' out of town as hard as you could. Seems you'd just killed a man over a difference of opinion on how much a horse cost. The man you killed thought it was worth forty dollars . . . but as I recall, you took it for nothin'."

"I'm gonna take you in, Hunter."

Hunter's hand was poised at the ready just over the butt of his own pistol. "Now why would you want to do somethin' like that, Marshal?," he snickered. "I mean us bein' old friends and all." His smile broadened. "Why, now that I come to think of it, I was ridin' hell-for-leather out of town with you that same day. I guess we're just alike, you and me. We ain't neither one of us lived what you'd call a lily-white life."

It was Josh's turn to smile. "Could be that you're right," he admitted. "But you see, I got a copy of a letter that the territorial attorney general sent out to all law enforcement officials askin' that you be picked up if you were spotted. As a matter of fact, he authorized a good-sized reward for you. I'm taking you in, John."

"For the reward?"

Josh shrugged. "A man has to make a living."

"I may as well tell you, Josh. I'm not goin' peaceable. If you want me, you're gonna have to kill me."

"It doesn't have to be that way," Josh suggested. "You could give yourself up; have your day in court."

"Haw! Fat lot of good that'd do me. There was at least half-a-dozen witnesses seen me and Pete gun down them two bank tellers. We go to court, we're gonna hang."

Nodding his head slowly, Josh agreed, "Yeah, I guess you might be right."

"So I reckon I'd rather just get it took care of here," Hunter went on.

"I figured as much," Josh sighed. He flexed his fingers. "I'll give you first move."

Hunter's smile was strained. "You're doin' that for me for old time's sake, are you, Josh?"

"For old time's sake," Josh replied, nodding.

"Well, I guess there ain't no way of gettin' around it," Hunter said. He quit talking and stared at Josh, his fingers jerking nervously.

The silence grew until it was almost palpable. As the tension mounted, Jared happened to glance at the gilt-edged mirror. In it, he saw Pete at the top of the stairs, leaning over the railing and taking very careful aim at Josh Wade. The agent could tell from the expression on Pete's face and the tension in his hand that he was not merely backing Hunter up—he was about to get the drop on Josh Wade.

"Marshal, look out!" Jared called.

Frustrated by the warning shout, Pete turned his gun on Jared. "You squealin' son of a bitch!" he bellowed, pulling the trigger as he did so.

Katie suddenly seemed to realize what was happening, and she braced herself against the wall of the staircase and began screaming.

Jared immediately dropped his beer and, leaning to one side, pulled his pistol, shooting just as Pete did.

The slug that Pete fired from the balcony tore through the top of the bar exactly where Jared had been standing, then ripped into the glasses Sam had stored on the shelf. Pieces of glass flew from behind the bar like shrapnel from an exploding shell. Pete fired again, and the second shot shattered the mirror and it fell, leaving only a few jagged shards hanging in place.

Jared's single shot was discharged with deadly accuracy, for Pete suddenly dropped his pistol and grabbed his throat. He stood there stunned, clutching his neck as blood oozed between his fingers. Then his eyes rolled up into his head and he twisted and fell, sliding head first down the stairs and following his clattering pistol all the way to the bottom. He lay motionless on the lowest step, his open but sightless eyes staring vacantly up at the ceiling.

While everyone's attention was riveted on the battle between Jared and Pete, Hunter went for his own gun. Jared was still looking at the man he had killed when he heard the roar of another Colt. Though it had seemed to Jared that time had stilled, the interplay between Hunter and Josh took place almost simultaneously with his own battle.

With the marshal's attention diverted to Pete for just a heartbeat when Jared shouted, Josh very nearly lost his own life, for Hunter took that opportunity to fire. But Hunter's shot was badly placed, and the .44-caliber bullet whistled through the crown of the lawman's hat, whipping it off his head but doing no further damage.

Recovering quickly from his moment of distraction, Josh Wade returned the gunman's fire so quickly that the two shots he got off sounded like one. One of the slugs struck Hunter in the forehead, and the impact of it knocked him backward onto a table where he lay belly-up, his head hanging down on the far side while blood poured out of the hole in his forehead and puddled beneath him. His gun fell from his lifeless hand and clattered to the floor.

The marshal then swung his pistol toward the men who had been playing cards with Hunter and Pete. "I know you, Dingus, Bates, and you, Tony. You're all from the Rocking S, aren't you?" the lawman asked menacingly.

"Yeah," one of them confirmed.

"You want part of this?"

"Hell, no!" Tony shouted, throwing his hands up in fear. "Good Lord, don't shoot us!"

"Marshal, we may work for the Stockards, meanin' we ain't exactly best pals with you," Dingus said calmly, "but that don't mean we're with these fellas. Hell, we never seen 'em before they rode in today."

"They're tellin' the truth, Marshal," Sam called from behind the bar.

Jared Macalester heard rapid footfalls on the wooden walk outside and looked toward the entry, which was partially obscured by the large, acrid cloud of gun smoke wafting toward the batwings. Then Billy and Adam Wade, their deputy marshal badges gleaming on their chests, pushed through the swinging doors and stepped through the pall of smoke, both carrying shotguns. Though Jared had not met Adam yet, he could discern enough of a resemblance to Josh and Billy to realize who he was.

"You all right, Josh?" Billy asked.

"Yeah, I'm fine."

"Who's this fella?" Adam Wade asked, swinging his shotgun toward Jared.

"He's all right," Billy explained quickly. "That's Jared Macalester, the trackwalker."

Walking over to Jared, Josh clapped him on the shoulder. "Yeah," the marshal announced, "fact is, I wouldn't be alive without him. He saw Pete takin' a bead on me from the top of the stairs."

Adam strode across the room to Pete's body and knelt beside it, looking at the wound in the throat. Then he glanced up toward the top of the stairs where Katie was still standing, rooted to the same spot and silent now but still too terrified to move.

Turning to Josh, Adam smiled at him admiringly and declared, "Big brother, that was a pretty good shot you made, takin' this fella down from the top of the stairs like you done."

"Not my shot," Josh corrected and pointed to Jared. "It was his."

"The trackwalker?"

"Yep."

"Mr. Macalester, when you made this here shot of yours, was you standing right where you are now?"

"Over there, by the bar," Jared answered, pointing to the bar where the bullet hole from Pete's gun was clearly visible.

Adam gave a low whistle. "I make that better'n sixty feet," he said. "Josh, wouldn't you make that about sixty feet?"

Josh estimated the distance, then nodded. "Yep, sixty feet or more."

"And you hit him square in the neck," Adam went on. "Mister, that's one hell of a shot for anybody. For a trackwalker, it's damn near unbelievable."

"I guess I got lucky," Jared said wryly.

Josh narrowed his eyes. "Maybe you did, and maybe you didn't. I'm beginnin' to wonder now just whose life I saved yesterday. Was it yours—or Tim Quick's? Maybe it's no wonder you didn't seem frightened by the idea of going up against him."

"Like I said, Josh, it was a lucky shot, that's all," Jared countered.

"Mr. Macalester," Adam put in, "with luck like yours, a fella don't need nothin' else."

Leaving his brothers to take care of things in the Bitter Drink, Josh bid Jared good night, picked up his Stetson and put the now-ventilated hat on his head, and left the saloon. Turning to his left, he began walking toward the depot, heading for the telegraph office. As he strolled along the boardwalk, he took long, deep breaths, trying to calm himself down.

It was always like this for him after a gunfight, the rapid heartbeat, the prickling along his spine. But it was not fear . . . it was exhilaration. He could not admit it to anyone—not even to his brothers—but he never felt more alive than he did right after he had killed someone.

John Hunter had been telling the truth: They had ridden out of town together that day. The two men had been on the dodge together for quite some time, sharing food, whiskey, horses—hell, they had even shared a woman once, back in Junction City. But that was then, and this was now. John Hunter was lying on the saloon floor with a bullet hole in his forehead, and Josh was about to send a message to Cheyenne, informing the attorney general's office that he had taken care of that "menace to society."

Reaching the depot, the marshal went inside and walked over to the telegraph counter where he greeted Carl Masters. He quickly composed his message and handed it to the telegrapher, standing beside the counter while Carl sent the message. The telegraph key clicked loudly, and Josh listened to every dot and dash, reading the words as quickly as Carl could send them. His ability to read Morse code was another secret he had shared with no one, and as marshal of Ironsprings, he sometimes found it advantageous to be able to read the telegraph messages without anyone knowing he could do so.

When Carl finished sending the message, he turned and asked the lawman, "Want to wait for a reply, Marshal?"

Shaking his head, Josh answered, "Nope, that's okay. I already know what the answer's gonna be. It can wait till tomorrow." He pivoted and headed back to the door, calling "'Night, Carl. See you in the mornin'."

Chapter 4

IT WAS EARLY AFTERNOON THE FOLLOWING DAY—THE DAY after what was now being referred to by the citizens of Ironsprings as "The Bitter Drink shoot-out." Taking a chair from his office out onto the shady front porch, Josh Wade sat down and tipped it back against the wall, folding his arms across his chest. From that vantage point, he could see with equal ease both the Bucket of Blood to his left and the Bitter Drink to his right, allowing him to watch everyone patronizing either establishment.

A couple of men were stringing a large banner across the street, while several more stood on the boardwalk, shouting conflicting directions to them. The banner read, in big, bold letters: GALA 4TH OF JULY CELEBRATION! COME ONE, COME ALL! FIREWORKS, FOOT AND HORSE RACES, BASEBALL GAME, AND DANCE!

Josh's gaze followed one end of the banner to where it was anchored at the Prufrock Hardware Store and

Undertaking Establishment. The two men killed in the shoot-out the night before were laid out in Max Prufrock's back room, being prepared for burial. By day's end, they would be interred in the least-desirable section of the cemetery, and a bill would be sent to the territorial capital for reimbursement. The marshal smiled to himself, knowing that Prufrock would charge the territory for two coffins and embalming—though in fact there would be no embalming, and all that would stand between the bodies and the dirt would be the piece of canvas they would be wrapped in.

Waving away a large horsefly that buzzed annoyingly around his head, Josh reached into his pocket and took out the telegram that had come from Cheyenne that morning. He reread it and smiled. The reward had been approved and could be picked up at the sheriff's office in Sweetwater, a town about twenty-five miles east of Ironsprings. The lawman had sent Adam there to claim the most generous reward, and when his brother returned, Josh Wade planned to celebrate.

He thought again about the shoot-out and the way Hunter's friend, Pete, had caught him by surprise. Josh knew that he should not have gone in to confront Hunter without taking one of his brothers with him, but he had known Hunter for a long time, and he knew he could take him if he had to. He sure had not planned on Pete taking a hand, and he was glad Jared Macalester had been there when it happened.

Josh had a few questions he wanted to ask Macalester when the time seemed right—such as where did he learn to shoot like that, and what was he doing in Ironsprings? So far, Jared Macalester had given him no real reason to worry, but Josh decided to keep his eye on the new man.

The town of Sweetwater, population 169, was made up of the usual collection of private residences and business establishments. Some of the buildings, by their substantial construction, showed a faith in the future of the town, while others were thrown together from canvas and scrap lumber, indicating that their owners were ready to leave at a moment's notice.

The most substantial building in Sweetwater was the Railroad Hotel, which, in addition to renting out hotel rooms, also served as a restaurant and saloon. Next door to the Railroad Hotel was the sheriff's office, and it was here that Adam Wade tied his horse.

As the lawman pushed open the door and entered the office, the sheriff looked up from his desk and smiled, recognizing his visitor. He leaned back in his chair and declared, "Well, Deputy Wade, I'll just bet I can guess what you're here for."

"Did it come?" Adam asked.

The sheriff opened the middle drawer of his desk and pulled out an envelope. "One thousand and five hundred dollars," he intoned. "Reward money to be paid for John Hunter. Too bad about the other fella, though. There was no reward on him."

"I reckon we'll just throw him in as a bonus," Adam chuckled.

"When you gonna make that town of yours legal?" the sheriff asked. "Seems silly that you have to come all the way over here to get your reward substantiated, just because you aren't incorporated."

"Maybe so," Adam responded, chuckling, "but on the other hand, if Josh was a marshal in a real town, we wouldn't be eligible for this reward, would we?"

"No, I reckon you got a point there," the sheriff laughed. He handed the money across his desk. "Don't spend it all in one place now," he teased.

"I aim to spend a little of it next door," Adam admitted, "then I'm gonna start back." Touching the brim of his hat, he said, "Much obliged for your help, Sheriff." Then he turned and headed out the office.

It took all of three strides for Adam Wade to reach the swinging doors that led into the saloon of the Railroad Hotel. He bellied up to the bar, and the bartender automatically started to reach for an open bottle of whiskey. But Adam waved him off and pointed to a full bottle. "If I open a new bottle, it's gonna cost you fifteen cents extra for the first drink," the bartender explained.

"I got fifteen cents," Adam assured him. "Open it up."

"You got it, mister," the bartender said with a nod, then pulled the cork and poured a glass.

Adam put a silver coin on the bar and held the glass under his nose. "Yeah," he sighed, "this is just what the doctor ordered."

After he tossed the drink down in one gulp, a sudden burst of laughter caused him to turn around. At a table near the cold potbellied stove, five men were playing cards. One of the players patted the young man to his right on the shoulder and proclaimed, "Mister, I'm sure glad you come along. You've brought me nothin' but good luck."

Adam stared at the young man, whose back was to him. "Johnny? Johnny Rogers, is that you?" the deputy finally asked.

The player swiveled in his chair and looked at the lawman, confirming that he was indeed the young man who worked for Charlotte Baker.

"Hi, Deputy," Johnny answered. Standing, he placed his folded hand on the table and told the others, "You fellas are gonna have to go on without me."

"Don't leave," the man to his left pleaded in mock despair. "I told you, you been bringin' me luck."

Johnny laughed. "I don't have no choice. I've already lost all my money." With a cheery wave, he walked over to the bar and ordered a drink.

"Let me buy that," Adam offered.

"Actually, I didn't lose all my money," Johnny confided. "Just the money I figured I could afford."

"That's a smart way to gamble, I reckon," Adam told the youth sincerely. "Might do me good to learn a lesson from you. You know, for a minute there, the way you're dressed and all, I wasn't sure it was you.

Come to think of it, I don't think I've ever seen you wearin' a gun."

Johnny looked down at his silver-studded vest, black pants, and hand-tooled black gun belt and holster and laughed. "That's because you're always seeing me in my working clothes. Mrs. Baker don't like me wearing a gun around a newspaper office, or when I'm delivering the papers. And I ain't gonna take a chance on getting ink on these clothes. This here is my traveling outfit. Say, how do you like my vest and hat? Pretty nice, don't you think?"

Nodding, Adam told him, "Not bad. But maybe a little too much silver for my tastes. Incidentally, what are you doin' over here in Sweetwater?"

"Mrs. Baker sent me. I had to run a few errands for her."

"Well, listen, I'll be startin' back in a few minutes. You wanna ride along with me?" Adam invited.

Johnny grimaced and shook his head. "Wish I could, Deputy, but I got quite a few errands to take care of yet," he replied. Tossing his drink down, he put the empty glass on the bar, then lowered his voice conspiratorially. "Fact is, I had no business being in this saloon in the first place. I'd appreciate it if you wouldn't mention it to Mrs. Baker, 'cause she's paying me extra to come over here, and she wouldn't like it much if she thought I was playing on her time."

"I won't tell a soul," Adam promised.

"Thanks. Well, I better get to my errands, else it'll be way after dark before I get back."

Adam watched Johnny leave, then ordered another drink.

"Mister, want to join us in a game?" one of the players at the table called.

Adam considered the offer. There was an empty chair, and he had some money. "Sure. Why not?"

Jared Macalester had been to the sites of the first two robberies and had found nothing. As he reached the site of the third robbery, some fifteen miles west of Ironsprings, he hoped his luck would be better. He slid from the saddle of the horse he had rented from the livery and ground tied the animal, then began looking around.

As he walked carefully all around the area, bending every now and again to investigate something that caught his eye, he reviewed the information he had. According to the report furnished by the Union Pacific, the train stopped for a bonfire that was built on the track. The four robbers then came out of the dark, and with two of their number holding their guns leveled on the engineer and fireman, the other two forced the mail clerks to open the mail car and throw down the money pouch. The thieves then slipped away and disappeared into the night.

After about an hour of careful investigation, Jared looked around and sighed with frustration. Other than the cross-ties being charred where the fire had been built, he had found nothing that was even remotely interesting or unusual. He walked over to his horse and was about to swing into the saddle when he caught the flash of something bright lying in the grass. Kneeling, he picked it up and saw that it was a silver concho—of the type Tim Quick had on his belt.

The Faraday agent stuck it in his pocket, and with a satisfied smile on his face, he mounted up, then started back into town.

Standing in front of the window of her newspaper office, Charlotte Baker watched impatiently for Johnny Rogers's return from Sweetwater because he was bringing some much-needed red ink back with him. Instead of seeing her assistant arrive, she saw Jared Macalester riding slowly into town, heading toward the livery.

It's about time he was out doing his job, she thought. *He's supposed to be a trackwalker, yet today's the first time I've seen him go out and check track.*

Giving up on Johnny, the redhead turned from the

window and started back toward her press. Then suddenly she stopped and, pivoting slowly, she looked back out the window toward the livery. "Wait a minute," she said aloud, her voice filled with curiosity. "Jared Macalester just came from the west . . . but the previous trackwalkers have always been responsible for the track to the *east* of town. What was he doing out there?" The question intrigued her, and she decided it was time to find out more about him.

Naked from the waist up, Jared Macalester was washing at the basin in his hotel room, cleaning up and getting ready to go to dinner. "Damn!" he suddenly swore loudly, getting soap in his eyes. Shutting them against the burning lye, he began groping for the towel that he knew was very near.

"Are you looking for this?" a woman's voice asked as a towel was placed in Jared's hands.

Starting with surprise and grabbing the towel, he quickly wiped his eyes, then opened them and found himself looking at the copper hair and smiling face of Charlotte Baker. She was wearing a light-green linen dress that Jared thought made her very enticing, and, for her part, she was obviously appraising his wiry, muscular physique.

"Is that better?" she asked with a lilt in her voice.

"Yes, thank you, Mrs. Baker." Looking at her questioningly, he then inquired, "But may I ask what you're doing in my room?"

"Well, I knocked and you said to come in."

"Oh?"

"Didn't you?"

Astonished at her boldness, he told her, "Frankly, I didn't even hear a knock."

"Oh, dear!" the redhead responded, her eyes widening. "I'm so sorry—and so embarrassed."

"I accept your apology," he assured her, a smile forming on his mouth, "but I find it hard to believe you're embarrassed."

"You're right," Charlotte laughed. "It's hard to

embarrass a widow, just because she happens to walk in on a man without his shirt."

Jared pointed to a ladderback chair, the only chair in the room. "As long as you're here, won't you sit down?" he invited.

As his guest sat, the agent pulled open the top drawer of his chiffonier and took out a couple of shirts, one green and one blue. He looked at both of them, weighing the merits of each, then started to put the blue one back in the drawer.

"No, wear the blue," Charlotte told him emphatically.

With a smile Jared took her suggestion, putting the green one back instead.

"I apologize again," she said. "I suppose you think it's terribly forward of me to tell you which shirt to wear. But, you see, I got so used to choosing my husband's that it became a habit—and now, even though he's gone, seeing a man make a mistake on the shirt he's about to wear automatically brings that out in me."

"And I was about to make a mistake?"

"Oh, yes. The blue will look much better on you."

Jared put on his blue shirt and began buttoning it. Amused by this sudden turn of events, he found it impossible to keep the grin off his face. "Tell me, what can I do for you, Mrs. Baker?"

"Charlotte, remember?"

Nodding, he agreed, "Right. What can I do for you, Charlotte?"

She smiled. "That's much better. Well, Mr. Macalester—"

"Jared, remember?" he cut in.

Laughing, she continued, "Well, Jared, I haven't properly thanked you yet for coming to my rescue on the train, and I would like you to be my guest for dinner tonight. I do hope you accept, because I've already reserved a table."

"I'd be honored," he said. Turning away from her, he tucked his shirt inside his pants, then grabbed his jacket from a hook on the wall. He opened the door, then turned back to Charlotte and offered her his arm.

"Shall we?"

"Indeed, we shall," she replied and giggled gaily.

They made their way along the hallway, then descended the stairs. Crossing the lobby, Jared was bewildered when Charlotte directed him away from the main dining room. Then, parting a beaded curtain, she led him to a table in a private dining room where they would be by themselves.

The room and the table setting were elegant—a surprise in such a one-horse town. Covered with a wine-colored damask cloth, the table held gleaming china, silver, and crystal, as well as an arrangement of fresh flowers. A candelabra sat on a sideboard, and its six perfect white tapers provided the light, casting a soft glow over the table and its occupants.

"Very pretty," Jared murmured as he pulled out Charlotte's chair for her. He then sat in a chair opposite her, feeling slightly out of place in such genteel surroundings.

Charlotte smiled. "I'm glad you appreciate it—though, unless I've forgotten everything I've ever known about men, I expect you'll be more interested in the food than in the utensils and such. I've ordered a roast in wine sauce. It's one of Millie's specialties. Have you met Millie?"

Jared smiled. "Yes, she served me breakfast yesterday. There was food enough to feed three men."

At that moment, the person in question entered, carrying an enormous tray laden with platters. Setting what was a virtual banquet before the two diners, Millie smiled and then made a discreet exit.

Groaning, the agent declared, "It's just as I feared. She didn't skimp any for this meal, either."

As she served both Jared and herself, Charlotte chuckled. "Millie feels that a well-fed man is a happy man—and she likes to keep her men happy."

"I've no doubt she does a good job," Jared said, staring at the mounds of food. He lifted the bottle of wine from its coaster and poured a glass for the publisher. His eyes held hers, his mind forming a question that he finally asked. "Now that we understand Millie, what about you? What do you think it takes to keep a man happy?"

Charlotte picked up her glass of wine and smiled over the rim at Jared. "Uh, uh, Jared," she chided. "I'm buying the meal, so I'm asking the questions."

"All right," he sighed. "Start asking."

Setting down her glass, she rested her chin on her hands and looked at him for a long moment before speaking. "I'll start by asking who are you?"

"Well, I thought you already knew. I'm Jared Macalester."

"Oh, I'm sure that that's your name," Charlotte quipped, "but who *is* Jared Macalester? Where did you come from?"

Jared took a sip of wine, then answered, "Originally from Charleston, Missouri—a small town in the southeast corner of the state. More recently, I've been drifting around out West . . . Dodge City, Boulder, Deadwood, Cheyenne—and now Ironsprings."

"You aren't really working for the railroad, are you?"

He leaned back in his chair and stared at Charlotte, assessing her, determining whether to confide in her. Remembering Matthew Faraday's instructions, he opted for half-truths. "Sure I am," he finally answered. "Why would you think not?"

The redhead smiled slyly. "For one thing, your performance in that shoot-out in the Bitter Drink Saloon yesterday. Some of the more morbidly curious citizens of our town have measured the distance of your shot. In case you're interested yourself, it was sixty-nine feet and seven inches. And, I am told by reliable sources that you made that shot while moving to avoid being shot yourself. You drew and fired without aiming, Mr. Jared Macalester, and you put a bullet not in the chest but in the neck of your adversary—who was not only firing at you, but was standing at the top of the stairs. That is a most impressive display."

"I suppose it was a good shot," Jared conceded.

"Are you working for the marshal? There are many who now think that you are."

"It would seem that I did serve his purpose, wouldn't it?" he replied, knowing that his oblique answer would not satisfy her.

"Are you?" she asked directly.

"No, I'm not. I told you, I'm working for the Union Pacific Railroad."

"What's a hogger?" Charlotte abruptly queried.

The sudden twist in her line of questioning surprised him. "What?"

"I want to know if you really are working for the railroad. If you are, you'll know some of the language. Now, what's a hogger?"

"A locomotive engineer."

"A string of varnish?"

"A line of passenger cars."

"The high iron?"

"The main track." Jared smiled. "Have I passed your test?"

"I'll admit that you know the language," she retorted, "but that doesn't prove anything since I obviously know the language, too—and I'm certainly not employed by any railroad."

Laughing, Jared conceded, "True enough. Well, I haven't always worked for the railroad," he admitted. "I've also been a city marshal a couple of times and a deputy sheriff once. I even worked for a while as a Texas Ranger."

"Ah ha!" Charlotte exclaimed, smiling broadly as if she had uncovered a deep secret. "Then one might say that you are a professional with your gun."

"One could also say that of anyone who has ever served in the army," Jared remarked. "Some twenty years ago, I fought for the Confederacy. Counting the others on my side, and the ones who fought for the North, I'd say there are a few million or so professionals with a gun around."

"That's not what I mean and you know it," Charlotte countered, her eyes narrowing.

"Then what do you mean?"

"You cannot be unaware that there have been a series of train robberies on the Union Pacific, all of them quite near Ironsprings."

Shrugging, he replied, "Yes, of course I'm aware of that. I do work for the railroad, after all."

"Would your presence here have anything to do with those robberies?"

Jared chuckled, "Surely you don't suspect me as one of the robbers?"

"If I did suspect you, I would hardly tell you that I did. How smart would it be to tell a dangerous criminal that you were suspicious of his activities? That is, assuming you were that dangerous criminal."

Jared chuckled again. He could not remember when he had enjoyed the company of such a quick, intelligent woman who was beautiful to boot. "And if I were involved with the train robberies, how smart would it be for me to admit it to you?"

Throwing up her hands, Charlotte laughed, "Touché. But you could be here as a result of the robberies and yet not be responsible for them."

The Faraday man knew what she was alluding to, but he played dumb. "I don't understand what you're suggesting."

"I'll come right to the point. You say you aren't working with Josh Wade. Well, then, are you a law officer for the territory of Wyoming or for the U.S. Government?"

"I've already told you. I'm a trackwalker."

"You say that, yet until today you had neither walked nor ridden one mile of track since coming to town. And today, when you did go out checking the track, you went the wrong way."

Jared laughed and stared at her. "The wrong way?"

Nodding emphatically, a look of triumph in her warm brown eyes, the publisher replied, "Yes, Jared, the wrong way. You see, the trackwalker who serves this region oversees the Bitter Creek to Ironsprings section of track. Bitter Creek is to the east. You have no business checking track to the west—unless you're looking for something other than broken ties and bent rails. Now, what were you looking for out there?"

He shook his head, bemused. "You sure do ask a lot of questions," he muttered.

"That's my job," she reminded him. "So, Jared, what do you actually do for the railroad? Are you a railroad detective?"

"You were right about this roast," he responded, taking the upper hand. "It is delicious."

"Am I to take it by that remark that this interview is finished?" Charlotte asked.

Grinning, he peered at her and responded, "Why? Would that mean I couldn't finish my dinner?"

Charlotte laughed. "Go right ahead. Eat and enjoy. You may have already told me more than you intended."

"Then in that case, may I ask a few questions of you?"

She smiled self-consciously. "I suppose so."

"Tell me what you know about Ike Stockard."

It was clear from the expression on Charlotte's face that she had been expecting a far more personal line of questioning. Recovering quickly, she replied, "Ike Stockard? He's a rancher."

"A successful one?"

"You might say that. He and his two brothers, George and Charley, have a fifteen-thousand-acre spread just west of here."

"Good stock?"

"Yes. And he has good water and good grazing land besides. His father was one of the first people out here, so he got the choicest land."

Jared paused briefly before asking his next question. "Did he ever swing a wide loop?"

Charlotte smiled wryly. "Well, now, Jared, what rancher in Wyoming hasn't? As I understand it, in the old days, the cattle were just turned free to graze, and they essentially became joint property. Whoever was able to round up the most came out ahead."

"That's not acceptable now, though?"

Toying with her fork, the redhead shook her head slowly. "No, not at all. While people might wink at someone who rustled a few cows in the past, it is definitely frowned on today."

The agent leaned toward Charlotte and lowered his voice. "I heard someone down at the depot say Ike might have been involved in a stage robbery."

"Someone down at the depot talks too much," she muttered sharply.

"Then there is something to the story?"

"I don't know," Charlotte sighed. "Before the bank we have now there was a bank called Western Trust." She gave a scornful laugh. "Some trust. All the while they were actually transferring the depositors' money to Denver. Then the bank conveniently 'failed,' and a lot of people lost a lot of money. Ike Stockard had just made a sizable deposit. Shortly thereafter, a stagecoach carrying money from a bank owned by the same people was stopped and robbed."

Jared had to ask the question. "By Ike Stockard?"

Shrugging, Charlotte replied, "No one has ever proved that. There were three men, all of whom wore masks." Her eyebrows rose, and she added, "The interesting thing is, the amount of money they took was exactly equal to the amount the Stockards lost. The rest of the money shipment—more than half—they let go through."

"You're right, that is interesting." He paused, weighing all she had told him, then asked, "What can you tell me about Josh Wade? I gathered from the few words he exchanged with John Hunter that he's had a pretty checkered past of his own."

"I wouldn't doubt it," Charlotte allowed. "Most of his kind have. And in truth, the way he's running this town now borders on criminal. You want to know what I was most surprised about by the gunfight yesterday?"

"What's that?"

"The fact that he actually fought with John Hunter." She sniffed derisively. "The only thing I can figure is that Hunter didn't pay Josh Wade enough to let him stay here."

The agent felt his pulse quicken slightly. "You really think Josh is accepting bribes from outlaws?"

"Why else would people like Tim Quick be here?" Charlotte replied.

"I don't know," Jared answered. "But I do know that there seems to be no love lost between Billy Wade and Quick. I saw the two of them together yesterday."

"Yes, well, Billy is the one factor in the equation I can't figure myself," Charlotte admitted. "The truth is, I don't think he's at all like Josh and Adam. I think if the other two would leave, Billy would probably make a pretty good lawman. And I think he would support incorporation, instead of fighting against it the way Josh does.

"And yet, if I understand it, Josh Wade and you . . . that is, he . . ." Jared felt himself getting uncomfortable and let the thought trail off.

"Josh Wade and I what?" Charlotte asked pointedly. "What are you implying?"

"Are you his woman?" Jared asked bluntly, finding himself surprised by the intensity of his tone.

"I am no one's woman, Jared Macalester, and I haven't been anyone's woman since Cap died."

He now was surprised by the relief he felt. "So then you would see other men socially? For example, if I wished to call on you, would you be receptive?"

Charlotte laughed gaily. "Good heavens, Jared, are you asking permission to come courting?"

Jared felt his cheeks color. For all intents and purposes that was exactly what he was asking—however, he was also interested in the information he could get from her . . . though, of course, he would never tell her that. Smiling, he said, "Yeah. Yeah, I guess I am at that."

To his surprise, the smile she gave him was somewhat shy. Then, in a clear effort to ease the slight awkwardness of the moment, she turned her attention to her dinner.

Following her lead, Jared began in earnest the formidable task of tackling his enormous meal.

Chapter 5

AS JARED MACALESTER WANDERED AROUND IRONSPRINGS over the next several days, he decided that it was a good thing that he had made the connection with Charlotte Baker, because it had become much more difficult for him to gather information. Conversations had a tendency to stop whenever he appeared. At first he feared that someone had found out who he really was—but then he realized that that was not it at all. People stopped talking when he came around because they were afraid of him.

Before the gunfight, Jared had been thought of as the trackwalker, someone who merely blended into the background, unnoticed by people exchanging the latest news and gossip. But his performance in the saloon had changed all that, moving him out of the background so that now, no matter where he went, he was noticed immediately. This, he knew, was the kind of notoriety men like Tim Quick craved; the agent, however, found it not only distasteful but inconvenient as well.

As he and Billy Wade shared a table in the restaurant at the Cattlemen's Hotel, he mentioned to the deputy the way people were now reacting to him.

Billy laughed. "Yeah, I'm afraid that's the price you pay. The bad thing is, folks make no distinction between people like us and someone like Tim Quick. To them we're all the same: gunmen, shootists, pistoleers. They see no right or wrong to what we do."

"They're quite correct," a familiar voice behind them declared.

Jared looked over his shoulder to find Josh Wade standing there. Walking around to the other side of the table, the marshal pulled out a chair and joined them, then signaled to the waitress. The woman started for the table, but before she even got there, Josh pointed to the blue-plate dinner special listed on the blackboard for twenty cents.

Picking up their conversation, Jared asked, "What do you mean?"

"I mean perhaps there is no right or wrong. Perhaps there's only life or death," Josh answered.

"Do you really believe that?" Billy demanded of his brother.

"Do you *not* believe it?" the marshal retorted.

"I don't want to believe it," Billy told him flatly.

Clapping the deputy on the shoulder, Josh announced with heavy irony, "Behold my brother—a man of ideals and principles."

"Come on, Josh, do you mean to say you've never had ideals or principles?" Billy asked.

"I reckon I did, once," Josh answered, his eyes staring blankly as if he was seeing something far away, "but when you've seen the elephant, boy, it's hard to keep hold of things like ideals and principles." He smiled then, and the faraway look went away. "I expect our friend, here, could talk about that—wouldn't you say so, Jared?"

"Maybe," Jared rejoined.

"Who are you, Macalester?" the marshal suddenly inquired.

The abrupt question took the Faraday man aback. "What?"

"Who are you? What are you doing here?"

"Josh, why are you asking him all these questions?"

"Because *he's* been asking a lot of questions," Josh answered. "All over town . . . or so I've been told. So I want to know who you are, and what you are doing in my town."

"Do you have any queries on me, Josh?" Jared asked.

"No," Josh admitted, "and don't think I haven't looked."

"Then why are you so concerned about it? I heard that as long as someone came to your town and kept his nose clean, you wouldn't cause him any problems. I haven't caused you any problems, have I?"

"No. No, you haven't."

Smiling easily, Jared promised, "And I don't intend to."

The marshal leaned back in his chair and peered at Jared as if gauging his character. Then he observed, "It's just that when a man who can shoot like you shows up, and I've never heard of you, I begin to get a little nervous."

"Josh, Jared's gun was on your side in that fight the other day," Billy reminded him.

"Not really," the marshal pointed out. "Pete was shootin' at him, not at me."

"He wouldn't have been shooting at me if I hadn't warned you about him," Jared countered.

"Maybe. But you've been spendin' a lot of time over at the newspaper office, goin' through old newspapers, bothering Charlotte Baker."

"Damn!" Jared exclaimed, grinning. "That's what this is all about, isn't it? You don't want me seeing Charlotte."

"Maybe I don't," Josh said, his tone sharp.

Jared looked at the marshal pointedly. "What do you plan on doing about it?"

"I think you ought to let it alone," Billy advised his brother.

"And I think you ought to get to work," Josh retorted as his blue-plate special was delivered. "There's a party at the Pleasure Palace tonight. I want you to keep an eye on it . . . kinda watch out for my interests."

Billy laughed. "Don't worry, big brother. I don't want you to have to buy any new red curtains or gilded mirrors for your whorehouse. Hell, if you have to do that, it'll probably wind up coming out of my salary." He finished his coffee, then stood up. Putting on his hat, he told the two men, "See you later," then turned and threaded his way out of the restaurant.

Jared watched Billy leave, then asked Josh, "I'd heard you own the whorehouse. So it's true?"

"Yes. And the Bitter Drink and half the Bucket of Blood."

"Being a marshal must pay a whole lot better now than it used to," Jared observed wryly, stroking his mustache.

"There are some advantages to wearin' a badge in a town that isn't incorporated," Josh explained, his eyes crinkling with amusement. "None of the tax money is wasted for such things as city improvements. All of it goes to pay for law enforcement." He chuckled. "That's me and my brothers."

"And the head tax you charge the ranchers for their cattle?"

"Haven't collected any of it yet," Josh admitted. "I just got the Administration Council to approve it a few weeks ago, and no one has shipped a herd yet."

"Will Ike Stockard pay it?"

"He will if he wants to ship his cattle," Josh said resolutely.

While Jared and Josh were finishing their meals, George and Charley Stockard—Ike's two younger brothers—along with two of their ranch hands, were in the process of getting roaring drunk at the Bitter Drink Saloon. They had been looking for trouble even before they arrived, passing a full bottle of whiskey between them that was empty by the time they reached the town limits. Deciding to show the Wades that they had the right to come to town any time they wanted to, they were surly and aggressive when they first walked into the Bitter Drink, and with each new drink they got progressively louder and more obnoxious.

"Where's that damned Josh Wade?" George shouted, putting down the whiskey bottle he had been drinking directly from. "Hey, Sam, have you seen the marshal anywhere?"

"Not since early this evenin', Mr. Stockard," the bartender answered. "Why do you want to see him?"

"It's more like I want Josh Wade to see us," George slurred. "I want him to know that anytime—" He abruptly stopped and hiccupped, and the others with him laughed.

"You're drunk," Charley declared.

"I'm not drunk," George insisted, brushing his lank brown hair out of his eyes. "I've just got the hiccups, is all. Can't a fella have a case of the hiccups without you sayin' he's drunk?"

"Not if he's really drunk," Charley rejoined in a sing-song voice, and though it was funny to no one else in the saloon, it was hilarious to the four men who had come in from the ranch.

George slammed his bottle down, gesturing for a new one. "Yeah, well, anyway, I want Marshal Josh Wade to see us in his town."

"In his saloon, even," Charley boasted, smiling broadly and showing the gap between his front teeth.

"And with his women," Dingus added. He looked around the saloon then, and noticed that there were no bar girls present. "Hey!" he called, his gray eyes narrowing. "Where's Katie? Where's all the purty women?"

George lifted the new bottle to his lips and took several swallows as he looked around. Looking back toward the bartender, he whined, "Dingus is right, Sam. There ain't no women down here. Where are they?"

"They're all down at the Pleasure Palace tonight. There's a big party down there, and they needed all the girls they could round up."

"A party? Well, hell, I like parties," George laughed. "Don't you like parties, little brother?"

"Yeah, I like parties," Charley agreed. "What about you boys? Don't you like parties?"

"Sure, we like parties," Dingus and Bates answered in unison.

George smiled broadly, took another swallow from his bottle, then passed it around to the others. "Well, then, why don't we go to the damned thing?" he suggested. "There sure ain't no women here."

"Mr. Stockard, I wouldn't do that if I was you," Sam advised, wiping up a puddle of whiskey that spilled from George's bottle.

"Oh? And why not?"

"It's a private party."

Glaring at the bartender, the rancher sneered, "A private party, huh? Well, let me tell you and this whole damn town that if I want to go to the Pleasure Palace, I'll damn well go to the Pleasure Palace." He slapped his whiskey bottle onto the bar and cackled, "Come on, boys, let's go down there and pick out the best-lookin' whores in the place."

"Hell, why not?" Charley agreed. Picking up the bottle, he took one final swig, then casually tossed it over his shoulder. It hit the corner of the bar and smashed into little pieces, but the four men heading out through the swinging doors did not even turn around.

"There's gonna be a shootin' for sure," Sam growled as he began sweeping up the shards of glass.

"Sure is," one of the patrons agreed.

"Come on, let's go down there and watch," another

patron suggested, and a moment later there was a mad rush for the door.

As the Stockards, Dingus, and Bates walked unsteadily toward the Pleasure Palace, word spread from building to building along Front Street about what was going on. People began spilling out into the street and hurrying to watch the show. By the time the foursome reached the Pleasure Palace, half the town had turned out and was gathered in front of the building.

The crowd was lit by a gas streetlamp that sputtered and hissed on a nearby pole. It cast a golden bubble of light out onto the street, making deep shadows on the faces of everyone present—although the look of expectancy everyone wore was easy to discern.

Word of the Stockards' coming had reached the Pleasure Palace even before they did. As a result, Josh Wade and his two brothers were standing on the front porch, waiting for them and their cohorts.

"I believe you gentlemen know that you've come to a place where you aren't wanted," Josh said, his arms folded across his chest. He spoke in a low, quiet voice, all the more menacing because of its lack of emotion.

Jared Macalester, like everyone else drawn to the Pleasure Palace by the spreading word, stood in the semidarkness, watching as the drama began to unfold.

"Get out of the way, Wade," George called out. "Me and my friends is comin' in." In contrast to Josh Wade's voice, his was loud and threatening—and fearful. George, as were all the men with him, was clearly jittery and appearing even more so in light of Wade's deathly calm.

"You got that, Josh Wade? We're comin' in," Charley bellowed, the anxious look on his face revealing the effort he was making to keep his voice from breaking in fear.

"No, I don't think so, Stockard," the marshal answered, as calmly as before.

"What makes you think we ain't?" Charley countered belligerently.

Drawing himself up, Josh warned, "Because I aim to stop you."

"The only way you gonna stop us is to shoot us," George proclaimed, his words slurring.

"I'm prepared to settle matters once and for all in just that way," Josh announced as he dropped his arms loosely by his sides.

All conversation halted then, and there was a collective holding of breath as the crowd waited for the next move. Everyone realized that what had started out as an evening of boisterous revelry for the Stockards was about to end in a shoot-out. If so, it would be disastrous, for even sober, the Stockards and the two cowboys with them would be no match for the Wades —and they definitely were not sober. In fact, Charley Stockard was so drunk that it was all he could do to stand on his feet.

One man in the crowd muttered, "Hell, them boys is so drunk, if Josh Wade and his brothers draw on 'em, it'll be legalized murder."

Jared Macalester turned and stared at the man who had spoken, then looked back at Billy Wade and saw the pained expression on his face. "I'd say you're right, mister," the agent told the man from the side of his mouth. "But it looks to me like Billy's going through a private hell. If shooting starts, he'll have no choice but to stand with his brothers—but it's damn clear that it's not something he wants to do."

Suddenly Jared started pushing his way through the crowd until he was standing right behind George Stockard. Then, so quickly that few in the crowd saw what he was doing, he pulled George's pistol from its holster and brought it crashing down on the rancher's head. George dropped like a sack of potatoes.

When Bates and Dingus saw that George was down, they suddenly lost their own taste for fighting, and they threw up their hands.

"We ain't gonna draw, Wade!" Bates promised. "We ain't gonna draw!"

Looking down at the prostrate form of his adversary, Josh's jaw muscles clenched and unclenched. For a brief moment it appeared as if he were going to draw anyway, but then he relaxed. Shifting his gaze to Jared Macalester, Josh gestured at the unconscious form of George Stockard and barked, "What the hell'd you do that for?"

"Well, now, it looked to me like there was about to be a fight," Jared replied, his voice easy and calm, "and I thought that might be a way to stop it."

"Yeah, well, you didn't stop it. You just delayed it," Josh muttered.

"What are you talking about, Josh?" Billy asked anxiously. "You don't mean you're just gonna wait till George comes to?"

"No, I don't mean that," the marshal grumbled. "But there'll be another time he or one of his brothers —or maybe even all of 'em—will come at me. And at that time the party will commence again. Seems to me like it would've saved a lot of worry and time if I'd just gone ahead and killed him here and now."

Adam tapped his brother's shoulder. "Stockard's comin' around, Josh. What do you want to do with him and the others?"

"Take 'em out to the edge of town and turn 'em loose," Josh spat.

Tim Quick suddenly hooted from just inside the door of the Pleasure Palace. "Why don't you let 'em come on in, Marshal?" he taunted. "The girls in here will take care of 'em."

"Yeah," Grub added, "we can get Big Betsy to drop one of her tits on 'em. That'll hold 'em down all night."

The crowd laughed, but Josh turned to the taunters and pointed toward the inside of the building. "Get back inside there now," he told them menacingly, "or *you'll* spend the night in jail!"

"We're goin', Marshal, we're goin'," Quick promised, holding up his hands in mock fright. "Just wanted to offer you help if you needed it."

Ignoring him, Josh Wade turned to his brother and ordered, "Adam, you and Billy take the Stockards and their hands on out of here."

"All right, Josh. Come on, you men. Let's go."

With Billy supporting the still-unsteady George and Adam holding up the slightly more composed but very inebriated Charley, the four cowboys were led down the street away from the Pleasure Palace.

They had gone only a few paces when Josh called from the porch of the Pleasure Palace, "Oh, and you Stockards, if I see you again tonight, there's gonna be hell to pay."

George stopped in his tracks, but Billy grabbed him by the collar and propelled him along.

"This won't do you any good, Billy Wade," George blurted as Billy persistently marched him toward the edge of town. "Soon as you let us go, we're comin' back."

Tightening his grip, Billy growled, "You heard what my brother said."

"I don't give a damn what your brother said. The only way he can stop us is to kill us."

Sighing with frustration, the deputy pointed out, "George, you know damn well he can do that, if it comes to it."

"Maybe he can and maybe he can't," George slurred, stumbling slightly. "We can pull a trigger, too, you know."

Suddenly Bates looked at his employer and declared, "George Stockard, Lord knows I'm on your side—but I don't mind tellin' you, I'm just as glad we didn't have to go up against Marshal Wade tonight."

"Now you're talking like a sensible man," Billy told him.

"Now he's talkin' like a coward," George hissed. He then challenged, "I aim to get this settled, tonight."

Drawing to a halt, the deputy turned and looked his charge square in the eyes. "No, you aren't," Billy replied, "because I'm going to stop you."

"How're you plannin' on doin' that?"

"By throwing you in jail." Changing direction, he started dragging George to the marshal's office.

Dingus threw up his hands and said, "Deputy, I ain't got no stomach for spendin' any time in jail—'specially when I ain't done nothin' to cause it."

Shaking his head, Billy responded, "I know that, and I'm not talking about you and Bates. Just George and Charley. You two go on out to the ranch and tell Ike he can pick up his brothers first thing in the morning."

The two ranch hands looked at each other and nodded. "Sure thing, Deputy," Dingus agreed. "Sure thing."

Turning on their heels, the two men headed as quickly as they could for their mounts, which were still tied in front of the Bitter Drink Saloon.

Adam watched them go, then prodded Charley toward the jail. "Don't worry, Stockard," he told the rancher. "You'll have a nice, restful night. We Wades'll guarantee it."

Later that evening, Jared Macalester was standing at the bar in the Bitter Drink, sipping a beer, when Billy Wade came in. Calling the deputy over, the agent asked, "Did the Stockards get out of town all right?"

"Actually, I didn't take them out of town," Billy replied. "George started talking big about how he was going to come back and take care of Josh—so I figured the best way to keep him and his brother alive was to put both of them in jail."

Nodding, Jared allowed, "You're probably right. How'd they take it?"

Billy laughed. "They complained a little at first, but they were so drunk they passed out as soon as they hit the cots in the cell. I'm sure they're still snoring peaceably. By the way, I came looking for you 'cause I wanted to thank you for what you did, breaking up the fight like that. I didn't know what I was going to do."

Humor flickered in Jared's eyes. "I'm sure Josh doesn't see my action in quite the same way."

"No, I guess not," Billy chuckled, "but you have my thanks. And if George and Charley were sober enough to know what went on here tonight, I figure you'd have their thanks, too."

Clapping the younger man on the shoulder, Jared said, "Well, I suppose you'll find out for sure in the morning."

"Yeah, I guess so," Billy breathed. "Well, I'd better be getting back to the office. Enjoy your beer."

"Thanks. And good night."

It was three o'clock in the morning, and Adam and Billy Wade were sharing the duty. Having finished his rounds half an hour earlier, the youngest Wade was relaxing, sitting behind the desk with his feet propped up. As he drank a cup of coffee, he watched his brother shuffling through a stack of wanted posters.

As Adam put another one of the fliers to one side, Billy joked, "Just exactly what is it you're doing? Picking out the ones with the biggest rewards?"

Oblivious to his brother's teasing, Adam shook his head solemnly. "What I was lookin' for isn't in here."

"And what would that be?"

"Nothin' worth talkin' about yet," Adam replied, his tone as vague as his words. Sitting up straighter in his chair, he then asked, "Say, Billy, what kind of reward you think the Union Pacific would give to someone who figured out who was robbin' their trains?"

"I don't know," Billy answered, shrugging. "They're a rich company, so I expect it would be a right smart amount. Why're you asking?"

"I think I know who it is. At least, I got an idea about who one of them might be."

All the humor drained from Billy's face as he asked his brother in a confidential voice, "What makes you think that?"

"It's somethin' I been studyin' on for the last two or three days . . . ever since I got back from Sweetwater." He abruptly shuffled the flyers together and put them back on the corner of the desk. "Sure wish I could've found what I was lookin' for in here," he sighed. "Would've made things a lot easier."

Silence fell between the two men, the only sound in the office coming from the steady ticking of the Regulator clock on the wall. After a few minutes, Billy stood up and stretched, saying, "Well, I guess it's time you made your rounds. While you're doing that, I'll go back and have a look at our prisoners."

Getting to his feet as well, Adam grabbed his Stetson from the peg and headed for the door. "How about a little game of checkers when I get back?" he asked over his shoulder.

"Good idea," Billy agreed. "I'll get the board set up."

Stepping outside, Adam squared his hat, then headed off, his boots echoing loudly on the wooden planks of the boardwalk. As he passed the alleyway between the leather goods store and Prufrock's, he thought he saw something move in the shadows. He smiled, figuring a drunk had taken refuge there to sleep it off.

Stepping toward the shadows, he asked, "What's the matter, partner? You too drunk to make it home? Well, I've been there a few times myself. You need some help?" Adam took another step toward the gap between the buildings.

A shotgun blast split the night, its two-foot wide flame pattern lighting for an instant both the broad smile on the face of the assassin and the shocked expression of the victim. A double-aught load of buckshot caught Adam in the chest, blowing open a hole big enough to see his lungs and heart. The charge threw him back into the street, where he landed flat on his back in a pile of horse dung, his arms thrown to either side and his eyes open but already sightless.

Somewhere nearby a dog barked loudly, but otherwise the town was silent.

The door to the marshal's office flew open and Billy Wade ran out into the street, his pistol in his hand. Heading up the street in the direction he was sure the blast had come from, he stopped running when he saw Adam lying in the street, and he cocked his pistol. He directed the revolver into the shadows of the alley, but, seeing no one, he went to his brother's side. Even before he knelt beside Adam, he knew his brother was dead.

"Who did this?" he demanded of the darkness. "Who did this?"

The dog barked again.

Gathering Adam's torn, lifeless body into his arms, Billy Wade wept.

Chapter 6

IKE STOCKARD ROSE FROM HIS BED, RAN HIS HAND THROUGH his light brown hair by way of combing it, then threw on his clothes. Stepping out into the hallway, he walked first to George's room, then Charley's, surprised to discover that neither bed had been slept in. He made his way to the kitchen and was just about to light a fire in the stove to make a pot of coffee when Dingus knocked on the door and came in.

"Mornin', Dingus. You seen either George or Charley around?" Ike asked, his voice still thick with sleep.

Nodding, the ranch hand replied, "Well, I know where they are. The Wades tossed your two brothers in jail for the night."

"Damn that son of a bitch!" Ike exploded.

"Actually, it was Billy Wade who done the tossin'," Dingus corrected, then peered closely at the rancher. "If you want to go into town and get 'em, I'll round up some of the boys and we'll ride along with you."

Ike sighed, and scratched his two-day growth of beard. "No," he finally decided. "Thanks, Dingus, but if we go in like Sherman's army marchin' into Atlanta, all hell'd break loose. I think it would be better if I went in alone."

"You're the boss."

When Ike threw open the door of the marshal's office and stepped inside later that morning, it was clear from the expression on his face that he had immediately perceived that something serious had happened. Josh Wade was sitting behind his desk looking extremely grim; Jared Macalester, who was leaning against the wall with his arms folded across his chest, seemed equally glum; and Charlotte Baker, who was there as well, appeared to be very saddened.

"Marshal, where are my brothers?" Ike asked. "Has something happened to them?"

Josh stood up, his face contorted in anger. Then he whipped out his gun and aimed it at Ike. "You've got a hell of a lot of nerve coming here, pretendin' you don't know what's happened!" he said angrily. "Did you think I'd just let somethin' like this go?"

"Let what go?" Ike asked, holding his hands out defensively. "What are you talkin' about? And why are you pointin' a gun at me?"

"I'm arresting you for murder," Josh barked.

At that very moment, Billy Wade stepped through the door, looking worn and drawn. "Josh, what are you doing?" the deputy asked, his voice weary. "You know damned well Ike didn't do it."

"Didn't do what?" Ike demanded. "Marshal, do you want to tell me what's goin' on here?"

"Put the gun away, Josh," Billy told his older brother quietly.

There was a long, tense moment. Then, with a frustrated sigh, the marshal put away his pistol.

"Ike, Adam Wade was killed last night," Charlotte spoke up, finally answering Ike's question.

"Killed? How? What happened?"

Jared Macalester pushed himself away from the

wall and stepped next to the rancher. "While he was making the rounds, someone was waiting in ambush alongside Prufrock's with a shotgun."

"Who are you?" Ike asked.

"Jared Macalester."

Ike's eyes narrowed. "Oh, yeah, Dingus and Bates told me about you. You're the gunman who sided with the marshal in that shoot-out in the saloon the other day."

Jared merely shrugged, and a heavy silence filled the room.

"Billy, did you get everything taken care of over at the undertakers?" Josh suddenly asked.

"Yeah," Billy answered, his voice breaking. "They're going to bury him this afternoon, like we want."

"This afternoon?" Charlotte questioned. "Oh, Josh, why so soon? There won't be time to put an announcement in the paper about the funeral."

"There won't be a funeral," Josh told her sternly. "Adam never was much for any kind of ceremony, so it'll just be a quiet, private burial. Billy and I will be there, but no one else."

Looking troubled, Ike declared, "Marshal, I want you to know that I'm truly sorry about your brother."

"I'm sure you are," Josh replied sarcastically.

"Well, I am, whether you choose to believe it or not," Ike countered. "But I'd like to know what makes you think I had anything to do with it?"

Josh glared at the rancher for a long moment, then answered, "We have an eyewitness who says it was George. You two look enough alike that, in the dark, the witness could've made a mistake."

"George? Wait a minute! Are you tellin' me George did this?"

"No," the marshal snapped.

"But you just said—"

"George couldn't have done it," Billy interrupted and pointed to the back of the building. "He and

Charley were already in jail when this happened. As a matter of fact, I was with them when I heard the shot."

"Who's the person who identified George?" Ike demanded.

When neither lawman answered, Charlotte spoke up, admitting, "We don't know. This morning, Johnny found a note on the door of the newspaper office." Reaching over to the marshal's desk, she picked up a folded piece of paper and showed the note to Ike, which read:

IF YOU WANT TO KNOW WHO SHOT THE DEPITY IT WAS GEORGE STOCKARD. I KNOW THIS BECUS I SEEN IT

Shaking his head, Ike muttered, "You're goin' by some anonymous note? Hell, this don't prove a thing. Why, this couldn't prove George did it even if he hadn't been locked up at the time."

"No, but it can make a fella suspicious," Josh Wade remarked. "There's bad blood between us, Stockard. I figure you wouldn't be all that upset if something happens to one of us."

"Marshal, if it ever comes down to it, you and me'll do our shootin' face to face," Ike promised. "I won't be hidin' in a dark alley somewhere. Now tell me, why are my brothers in jail?"

"Let's say it's for disturbin' the peace," Josh said. "But if you want 'em, you can have 'em. Billy, turn 'em loose."

"Sure thing." Billy got up and walked over to the wall where the big key ring hung on a hook.

"You were stretchin' it a little, weren't you, Deputy, puttin' them in jail for disturbin' the peace?" the rancher queried. "Ordinarily, you'd send 'em home." Cocking his head, he added, "You know, it surprised me a little, Billy, when Dingus told me it'd been you who locked Charley and George up. I always sort of figured you was cut from a little better cloth. Why'd you think it necessary to put them in jail?"

"To keep me from killin' 'em," Josh barked.

"What?" Ike's hands started automatically for his weapon.

"Ike, it isn't as you think," Charlotte quickly interceded in a calm, rational voice. "Your brothers were very drunk . . . and challenging. They were trying to provoke the marshal into a gunfight."

Relaxing, the rancher mumbled, "I see." Ike looked at Billy and nodded. "In that case, I reckon you did the right thing after all."

Billy then went into the back and returned a moment later, leading Ike's two brothers, who looked painfully hung over.

"You boys ready to go home?" the elder Stockard asked.

"Yeah," Charley groaned. "I've seen about enough of the Wades to last me a good long while."

The three ranchers started for the door when Josh's voice stopped them.

"Stockard, next time you or your brothers come into my town and cause trouble, you'll be doing more than spending the night in jail."

"I'll see you around, Marshal," Ike replied laconically, propelling his brothers out the door, then shutting it hard behind him.

As soon as they were gone, Charlotte shook her head and sputtered, "Josh Wade, you can't go around threatening citizens like that."

"Sure I can," Josh snorted. "I'm the marshal, remember."

"You're the marshal only as long as Ironsprings remains an unincorporated town," Charlotte countered angrily. "Believe me, I'm doing all I can to fix that."

"I'm sure you are, Charlotte Baker, I'm sure you are," Josh growled, picking up his hat. "If you'll excuse me, I have to make my rounds now. In case you haven't noticed, my police force has been reduced by a third. I imagine that should make you very happy."

"Josh!" Charlotte gasped, looking horrified. "You know better than that."

"Do I?" Josh replied with a sneer, looking first at her, then Jared. Striding across the office, he yanked open the door and walked out, leaving Charlotte, Jared, and Billy staring after him.

"Charlotte, don't pay Josh any mind," Billy apologized. "He's upset over Adam's murder."

"Well, Lord knows he has a right to be," the redhead sighed. "But he's wrong in thinking that I don't care. We're all upset about Adam, Billy. I might have a difference of opinion about how things should be run around here, but I'm truly sorry about your brother. I just can't understand who would do such a terrible thing."

"Have you any idea who it was?" Jared Macalester asked.

"You know, I wonder if these train robberies—" Billy began, then stopped. "Ah, it's nothing," he then mumbled, dismissing the thought with a wave of his hand.

"It must've been something. Go on," Jared urged.

Billy stared blankly out the window, his eyes unfocused. "Well, it's just that Adam must've seen something or heard something recently. Last night, just before he went out on his rounds, he told me he had an idea who's been holding up the trains. But before I could ask him anything about it—" Billy paused "—he was dead."

"And you think whoever killed him might be the one responsible for the robberies?" the Faraday man asked.

Turning to face Jared, Billy paused a moment, then replied, "It does make you wonder, doesn't it?"

The third day of July dawned bright and clear, and after having a quick breakfast—practically forcing

Millie to give him only coffee and two eggs—Jared Macalester strolled over to the *Vindicator* office. Claiming that he owed her a meal, Jared invited Charlotte to have lunch with him. When she asked where she should meet him, he told her to be at the depot at about eleven.

"Eleven? Isn't that a little early for lunch? And besides, I've eaten at the depot, thank you, and that's not a place you go to enjoy a meal. It's only acceptable fare if you have to eat fast and get back on the train." She giggled, adding, "Besides, it's an odd day, so there isn't even a train this morning—meaning there isn't even any food available."

"Oh, but we aren't going to eat at eleven—and I wasn't planning on eating at the depot," Jared answered, being deliberately mysterious. "I've got something else in mind."

"What?"

"No, no, I can't tell you yet," he insisted, mischievously enjoying her confusion as she peered at him, trying to assess his self-satisfied grin. "It's a surprise. Just be patient, and you'll find out soon enough."

"Okay, I'm here," Charlotte said, when she showed up at the depot, promptly at eleven. "Now, what's the surprise?"

Jared smiled broadly, drawing out the suspense. "Just come this way, if you will, madam," he invited, leading her to the back side of the depot and across the side tracks where a solitary engine—green and red with shiny brass trim—sat waiting, blowing steam. The wheels were taller than Charlotte, and she had to look up to see the top of the rim.

"As you can see, I've already fired her up," Jared explained, "so we can get going right away."

She stared at him, disbelieving. "What? Jared Macalester, what on earth is this?"

"Well, specifically, it's a Hinkley and Williams two-four-zero," Jared replied. "The U.P. dropped it off so an extra engine would be available for the special runs tomorrow to bring in the watermelon, fireworks, beer, ice, and—if I'm not mistaken—the Green River baseball team and a group of its supporters."

Shaking her head in confusion, she remarked, "Well, I had heard that the railroad was going to make the engine available, but what do you mean you have it fired up so we can get going right away?

Jared laughed, relishing having topped her unexpected and elegant dinner for him. "That's the surprise. I've borrowed it so we can go on a picnic. I had Millie prepare us a picnic hamper, and it's already on board."

"You . . . you borrowed it?"

"Sure." He hooked his thumbs under imaginary suspenders and intoned, "This should prove that I work for the railroad." Leading her closer to the engine, he asked, "Have you ever ridden up front in the locomotive?"

"No, I haven't," Charlotte replied, her voice still incredulous.

"Well, I know it's supposed to be ladies first," Jared said, "but perhaps you'd better let me climb up ahead of you, and then I'll help you board."

"All right," Charlotte breathed.

After climbing into the cab, Jared stretched his hand down toward Charlotte's. As the redhead took his hand and strained to climb, her dress tightened against the curves of her body, and Jared eyed her with appreciation. Shifting his gaze before Charlotte noticed, he helped her into the locomotive.

Inside the engine there was a maze of pipes, valves, switches, and gauges. A small cushioned bench sat on one side of the engine cab, and an iron seat—like the ones on bicycles—was on the other side. Jared took the iron seat and began twisting a valve. "Sit down," he invited, pointing to the cushioned bench.

"Are you a hogger?" she asked, using railroad jargon.

"Well, we've already determined that at least I

know what the word means," Jared quipped. He turned a valve, and there was a sudden puff of steam. Jumping with surprise, he then started twisting the valve frantically until the steam stopped.

"Wrong one," he said, grinning sheepishly.

"Haven't you driven this engine before?" Charlotte asked in a somewhat tentative voice.

"Nope," Jared replied easily. He twisted another valve, and this time the steam was vented into the right place, and the train began to roll. "Ah, that's the one I need," he announced. He looked at Charlotte and smiled proudly, looking for all the world like a little boy who had finally done something right.

"Isn't it amazing," she said, "that simply turning that one valve could make this enormous engine move?"

"Yes, isn't it?"

"Which valve stops it?" Charlotte asked.

"Which valve stops it?" Jared echoed, puzzled. He looked around, scratching his head. "You know, that's a good question. I guess we really should know that, shouldn't we? I mean, in case we want to stop."

Charlotte laughed nervously as the engine picked up speed, leaving the town of Ironsprings behind them. "You are teasing, aren't you?"

"No, I'm quite serious. I mean, I know the thing will stop eventually, when it runs out of steam. But what if we wanted to stop suddenly? It would definitely be to our advantage to know how to do it." Assessing the various levers, he suggested, "Look around, will you? The brake is probably one of these levers or handles or something."

Charlotte stared at him. "Why are you asking me this? Where are the brake handles on other engines? Aren't they all pretty much alike?"

"I don't know," Jared stated. "This is the only engine I've ever driven."

"You mean—My God! You've never driven *any* engine before?"

"Nope. Ah," he said, putting his hand on a lever

and smiling broadly, proud of his accomplishment, "here it is. We're all set now."

"Oh, my God!" Charlotte groaned. "I'm with a madman! We're going to be killed!"

"No, we'll be all right," Jared insisted. He then laughed, "One thing for sure, we can't get lost, can we?"

"You're crazy," Charlotte declared.

"I'm crazy?" Jared hooted. "I didn't trust my life to someone who's never driven one of these things before."

Charlotte looked at Jared as if he were raving. Then apparently the outrageously bizarre humor of the situation struck her, and she began to laugh. She laughed so long and so hard that tears came to her eyes.

"I knew you'd be a good sport about it," Jared concluded, pulling on the whistle cord and adding to the merriment.

Charlotte managed to blurt out through her laughter, "What choice do I have?"

For the next half hour Jared worked hard at keeping the fire stoked by throwing chunks of wood into blazing flames in the firebox. He kept the throttle open all the way, racing the engine along the tracks at nearly forty miles per hour.

When the locomotive came out of a narrow gorge, the valley opened up wide before them, offering a picture-book setting of grassy fields, a sparkling stream, and huge old trees. Jared began twisting a number of valves, and finally he pulled the brake lever, bringing the engine to a halt.

"Time to eat," he announced. "Raise the cushion and look inside."

Charlotte jumped off the bench and lifted the cushion, discovering the seat was also a storage chest. Inside the chest was a picnic basket.

"Come on," Jared invited and pointed out the window, "there's a nice place over there, by the stream." Taking the basket from her hand, he started to climb down.

"Is it safe to leave the engine here?" Charlotte asked, leaning over the edge.

Jared chuckled. "Well, it sure isn't going to wander off like a horse might. And there aren't any more trains due till eight tonight." He helped Charlotte down, then escorted her to the rear of the tender where a burlap bag hung.

"What's that?" Charlotte asked.

"It's a trick I learned," Jared explained as he reached inside the bag, searching. "You soak a burlap bag in water, then hang it out and let the wind blow across it. As the wind causes the water to evaporate, it cools—Ah, here it is." He pulled out a bottle of wine and handed it to her. "Feel this. It's just as cold as if it had been buried in a snowbank."

She looked at him appraisingly. "Clever fellow." They started toward a small knoll, and Charlotte asked, "What else do we have for lunch?"

"Well, knowing Millie and her belief that no one should ever be hungry, I'd guess that whatever it is, there'll be plenty of it." He stopped and opened the basket. "Let's see. We have cold chicken and roast beef, potato salad, sliced cucumbers, baked bread, and a whole cake." He looked at her and laughed. "That should hold us till dinner time."

Charlotte spread out the red and white checked tablecloth that Millie had thoughtfully folded in the basket, then set out the food. There were two glasses in the basket, and Jared filled them with wine, handing one to Charlotte.

"Thank you, sir," the redhead said. "My goodness, Millie certainly outdid herself."

The Faraday man was delighted that everything had turned out so well, and admitted, "I asked her to do an especially good job because I was taking you on a picnic."

Charlotte chuckled. "Well, that explains it. She's

been trying to find another man for me ever since Cap died." She immediately blushed, putting her hand to her mouth. "Oh, dear! I didn't mean to make it sound as if I were hunting."

"That's all right," Jared replied gently. He held his glass up. "Let's drink this toast to the memory of Cap. He must've been a fine man to win you."

"He was," Charlotte murmured, and for a moment there was a distant, wistful look in her eyes as if she were recalling other times and other places. Then she smiled, and the look disappeared. "Thank you."

They drank the toast, then Charlotte gazed out across the valley. "You certainly chose a beautiful spot for our picnic," she told Jared.

The field before them waved with flowers of various hues and sizes. There were bold white and yellow ox-eye daisies, slender white and blue columbines, and brilliant red Indian paintbrushes. Beyond the valley, a great range of mountains rose.

"Sometimes," Charlotte mused, "when I spend so much time in town, I tend to forget how beautiful it is out here. I don't think I could ever live anywhere else." She then focused her attention on the repast before them, declaring lightly, "I guess we'd better get to this if we don't want to disappoint Millie."

They started eating the mounds of food, and for the next half hour they just enjoyed the meal and each other's company, saying little of any consequence. Then Jared took a folded-up newspaper from the hamper and showed it to Charlotte.

"I'd like to ask you a few things about this newspaper," he told her, regretting that he had to inject a serious topic into their picnic.

"About the *Vindicator*? Sure, go ahead."

Shaking his head, he noted, "Not about the *Vindicator*. About this particular edition. I've read every word in it."

Charlotte laughed. "Jared, don't tell me one of my scathing editorials has you upset?"

"No," the agent assured her. "Let me explain. This

edition was published on the same day as the train robbery where the guard was killed."

"What about it?"

"Do you know what time it was printed?"

The publisher brushed a lock of hair from her eyes and looked at him curiously. "Jared, why are you asking me all this?"

Jared hesitated, then handed her the paper. "All right, I don't suppose it would hurt to tell you. While I was checking the track—between Green River and Ironsprings—" he added with a smile, "I happened to come across this copy of the newspaper."

"I print almost three hundred papers a week," Charlotte quipped. "You're likely to find a lot of them."

"Yes. But this one is dated on the same day of the robbery . . . and I found it at the exact spot where the robbery took place."

"How do you know it was the exact spot?"

"I found signs there," he said, impatient at being interrupted. "Now, tell me, please, what time of the day was this particular paper published?"

"I'd say about four or four-thirty."

Jared stared at her for a moment, then shook his head emphatically. "That's impossible. There's no way someone could have left Ironsprings at four or four-thirty and gotten there in time. The robbery took place at about seven o'clock, and no one could have covered that distance in two-and-a-half or three hours."

"What if they went by train?"

"That edition was published on the third, remember? Westbound on the odd days, eastbound on the even? There was no eastbound train that day."

"Then that means the paper wasn't left there until after the day of the robbery—which means that the robbers didn't leave it," Charlotte concluded.

Jared suddenly felt more frustrated than he had since beginning the investigation. "Unless we can find some other explanation for it," he suggested.

"What other explanation can there be?"

"I don't know. But I intend to find out."

Looking at him suspiciously, she demanded, "Why? I thought you told me you weren't a lawman."

"I'm not. I'm a trackwalker," Jared lied. Seeing the doubting expression on her face, he ran his hand through his hair and sighed. "All right, the guard who was shot was a friend of mine," he explained. "I want to know who killed him."

Charlotte sat up straight and folded her arms across her chest. "And what if you find out? What will you do then? Kill the person who's responsible?"

"I hope it doesn't come to that," Jared said.

"Why don't you go to Billy with what you have so far?" she counseled.

"No."

"Why not? Maybe he has no authority outside Ironsprings, but he does have some experience. And he's not like Josh, believe me. I believe Billy is trying to do a good, honest job."

"I'd rather leave him out of it," Jared told her sternly, fearing he had already gone too far in taking her into his confidence. "And, Charlotte, you must promise me that you won't say anything to him about any of this . . . about the newspaper or even about my interest in the case."

"All right," Charlotte agreed, reluctantly. "If that's what you want."

"That's what I want." Looking at her, Jared suddenly felt an overwhelming urge to kiss her. Smiling, he added, "But it isn't all I want."

"What do you mean?"

"This is what I mean," the agent said softly. Putting his forefinger under Charlotte's chin, he lifted her face to his, then brought his mouth down to hers.

Charlotte's obvious initial surprise was followed by even more obvious enthusiasm, for she pressed her lips tightly against his, holding the kiss until he broke it off. When they finally separated, they looked into each other's eyes for a long moment, then Charlotte smiled and asked, "Is that all you want?"

"Maybe one more time," Jared suggested, and they kissed again until finally Charlotte pulled away from him. "Jared, no, we've gone far enough."

"We're just getting started," he countered, reaching for her again.

"No, please," Charlotte insisted. "I'm afraid that if you wanted to carry this further, I wouldn't be able to say no. It wouldn't be a fair fight just now."

Swallowing his disappointment, Jared studied her face carefully before he spoke. "All right," he agreed, "I don't want to push you into something you aren't ready for."

"You don't understand," she said, her voice poignant. "I might be more ready than you even want."

Puzzled, Jared stated, "I'm not sure I understand what you mean."

The redhead sighed, then said simply, "It's a woman's right to be mysterious." She then started repacking the picnic hamper, saying, "We really should be getting back into town."

"I guess you're right." He gazed into her warm brown eyes, trying to read them, then said, "Charlotte, at the Fourth of July celebration, I understand there's going to be a dance. Would you go with me?"

"Of course I'll go with you," she said easily.

"Good." He stood, then helped her to her feet. "I'll get the steam up and you'll be back at your office in no time." He glanced at the engine, facing away from town, then remarked, "It's good these things run just as well backwards as frontwards."

"I never realized that."

Chortling, Jared teased, "And you're the one who gave me the test on railroads."

Beginning early Independence Day morning, Ironsprings, like thousands of towns and cities all over the nation, had turned itself over to having fun. The celebration of the Fourth of July seemed to take on an even greater significance in the West, because the settlers in the area were desperate to hang on to some old roots. Out here, no matter how remote the town or village, the people had a feeling of not being alone because the party they were having was similar to those being thrown all across America, attended by every man, woman, and child.

Ranchers and their families, cowboys and their women, and cowboys by themselves who hoped to meet someone began swelling the streets of the town. Many came in wagons and buckboards, and many more rode—some on a horse they hoped would carry them to victory in the races that would be held later in the day. Everyone was putting his or her best foot forward, and all hostilities between the townspeople and the ranchers were set aside for the duration of the celebration.

At the quilting booth, the judges were having a very difficult time selecting the winner. Looking at the anxious faces of the crowd, composed of supporters of both the finalists—one a rancher's wife, the other the wife of a merchant—the judges knew that whomever they selected, half the people would be disappointed. Finally, making an inspired decision, the judges deemed it a tie, and both ladies walked away with blue ribbons.

Johnny Rogers won the horse race, which brought with it a prize of twenty-five dollars, and that had all the townspeople crowing for a while. But then the son of one of the ranchers won the foot race and a blue ribbon, and all the other ranchers hoisted him on their shoulders and gloried in his moment in the sun.

Everyone, however, shared the gloom over the baseball game. There had been one moment when the Ironsprings crowd, ranchers and townspeople alike, were able to cheer lustily, for Billy Wade hit a towering home run, sending the ball so far over the outfielder's head that he had not even retrieved the ball when Billy crossed home plate. But the victory was short lived, and the Green River Athletics beat the Ironsprings Knickerbockers rather handily by a score of eleven to one.

A fireworks display was held immediately after the sun went down, and then lanterns that had been hung around a wooden dance platform were lit. Held on a raised platform in an empty lot next to the livery stable, the dance was the highlight of the celebration. Music was provided by the volunteer fire department band, and when nearly everyone had arrived, the square dance caller raised his megaphone.

"Ladies and gents! Choose up your squares!"

Single cowboys started toward the young women, who, giggling and turning their faces away, shyly accepted their invitations.

A half-dozen sets were danced, and Jared Macalester had danced every one with Charlotte Baker. Then, as people regrouped for the next dance, Josh Wade claimed Charlotte for himself. Knowing that the marshal had expressed his admiration for the publisher, Jared was not surprised. However, he also knew that Charlotte did not return the lawman's feelings—although she was gracious enough to dance with him.

While the Faraday man stood off to one side of the dance platform, watching, a sneering, unpleasant voice hissed from the darkness behind him, "Well, Mr. Trackwalker, it looks like the marshal's got your girl." Turning, Jared saw Tim Quick in the shadows, leaning against the wall of the livery stable.

"It's a free country, Quick, and that's exactly what we're celebrating," Jared quipped. "She can dance with anyone she wants."

"Is that so? Well, then, maybe I'll give her a whirl."

"Except you," Jared added.

The gunslinger pouted. "What? Why now, I'm plumb put out that you won't let your girl dance with me."

"Yeah, well, that's just the way it is. I don't much like you, Quick. But then, I think you already know that." Tired of the conversation, Jared turned back to watch the dancers.

"I notice you ain't wearin' your gun tonight," Quick then remarked.

The man was right. He was not wearing his gun, and when the gunslinger pointed that out to him, the hairs on the back of Jared's neck stood up. He looked over his shoulder to see if Quick was wearing a gun. He was not. In fact, he was holding the hem of his coat out, showing that he was not armed . . . and he was smiling.

"I didn't have you scared, did I?" Quick mocked.

"Not much."

"You know, trackwalker, when you throwed me off that train, you caught me by surprise. I'd kind of like to get things square, if you know what I mean." He pointed to the dark behind the stable. "How about comin' back there with me to get this settled?"

"Go away," Jared shot back, turning away again. "I have more important things to do with my time."

"Well, Mr. Trackwalker, you might say that I'm not going to be put off. You see, if you don't come over behind the barn with me, I'm gonna whip you right here, in front of your girl and everyone. Now, folks is havin' such a nice time, I don't think they'd want the dance broke up by a couple of men fightin', do you?"

Jared sighed, hating the man for having gotten the better of the situation. "All right," he reluctantly agreed. "Let's get it over with."

As Jared followed Quick around the back of the barn, he kept a close eye on him, half expecting the cowboy to take him by surprise. What he did not expect was Quick's cohort, Tucker, to throw a punch as he reached the corner of the barn. But even though it came without warning, Jared managed to sense it in time to avoid its being a knockout punch. Nevertheless, it was a good hard blow, and the Faraday man felt his knees buckle slightly.

"Grub! Logan! Get him!" Quick called, and Jared was punched again, this time in the back of the neck.

But the shout had been enough of a warning so that this blow, too, was less damaging than it could have been.

There was very little light spilling back here from the lanterns around the dance floor, but in the yellow glow, Jared could see Quick grinning obscenely. The gunslinger doubled up his fist, getting ready to punch, but Jared managed to duck under it, then throw a counterpunch of his own. He caught Quick in the Adam's apple, causing him to gasp, but although it staggered him, he did not go down.

While Quick was recovering, Jared managed to score a telling blow to Logan's eye. Then he landed a punch to Tucker's mouth in which he felt a couple of the man's teeth go, and swinging an elbow into Grub's nose, he heard the cartilege crack, bringing forth a howl of pain.

Despite Jared's best efforts, however, he was unable to hold them off. Blow after blow was rained on him, and finally he reached the point where he could no longer punch back. All he could do was draw himself up into as tight a ball as he could and take the pummeling. Finally even that effort failed, and he went down. When he did, he was rewarded with a number of kicks.

After giving Jared one last kick, Quick slipped into the night with his cohorts. The agent lay still for several minutes. Then he cautiously moved first his limbs, then his torso. He felt extremely lucky, for he seemed to have sustained no broken bones, and there did not appear to be any internal damage. It was a severe beating and a painful one, but not one that was likely to leave him crippled for life. Opening his hand, he looked at the piece of silver that glinted in the dim light. He smiled slightly, wondering when Tim Quick would notice that he was missing a concho from his belt.

Deciding he could not lie there any longer, Jared summoned everything that was in him and managed to stand. He used the wall of the barn to support his progress and began a slow and painful trip back toward the dance floor.

He had almost reached his destination when he saw Charlotte coming through the milling crowd, looking around in confusion as if wondering where he had gone.

"Charlotte! Over here," he gasped, before falling forward and passing out.

When Jared opened his eyes, Charlotte was sitting on the edge of the bed, bathing his face with a damp cloth. Sunlight was streaming in through the window, and he was surprised that it was daytime. He then looked around the room and realized that he had no idea where he was.

"You are in the spare bedroom of my house," Charlotte explained, as if reading his thoughts. She dipped the cloth in a basin, rinsed it out, and placed it on his forehead. "How does that feel?"

"Better," he breathed, and even that slight effort hurt. "How did I get here?"

"Billy and Josh carried you. You were out all night." She looked at him sharply, then asked, "Who did it?"

"Tim Quick and his friends."

Sighing, she declared, "I thought as much. Billy thought so, too, but Josh wouldn't let him go after them. He said there was no proof. Well, now I can tell him—"

"No," Jared insisted, putting his hand out to stop her. "Don't."

"Why not?"

"I was invited back there," Jared admitted. "I didn't have to go. In a way, I'm responsible."

Charlotte got up and walked over to the chiffonier, picking up an envelope that she then brought back to the bed and showed to Jared. It was the letter he had received from Matthew Faraday about his assignment.

"I found this when I took your clothes off."

"You took my clothes off?" Shocked, Jared immediately reached under the sheet and realized that he was wearing only his underwear.

"I told you, I'm a widow," Charlotte laughed. "I've seen a man in his underwear before. Anyway, I couldn't clean you up without undressing you—and if ever I saw a man who needed cleaning, it was you." She shook her head, a wry smile on her lips. "Why ever did you choose a stable to have your fight?"

"I guess it was just handy," Jared sighed.

"I guess so." Her smile was one of resigned tolerance. "Anyway, I decided to wash your clothes as long as you were out of them, and this letter fell out of your pocket." She looked away from his piercing eyes. "I read it," she confessed. "You're a Faraday agent, aren't you? And Cedric Foster, the man who was killed in the train robbery, he was more than your friend. He was a fellow agent."

"Yes to both questions," he confirmed.

"And I still can't say anything to Billy?"

"No. Charlotte, since you read the letter, you know my orders are to tell no one. Please, you must keep my secret," he told her urgently.

"All right," Charlotte agreed, "on the condition you let me help you."

Jared smiled, feeling relieved. "At this point, I'll take all the help you can give me."

The redhead reached over to the top of the chest and picked up a small piece of silver. "You were clutching this so tightly I didn't think I'd be able to get it away from you," she said. "I recognize it. It's one of Quick's conchos. I figure you must have had some reason for wanting it, other than trying to deprive Quick."

"You're right." He looked around the room. "Where's my hat?"

"Hanging from a hook behind the door," she said. "I'll get it."

Charlotte brought him his hat, and he felt around under the lining until he located where he had put the small concho he had found at one of the robbery sites. Removing it from the hat, he held it alongside the piece of silver from Quick's belt.

"Damn!" he exclaimed, soundly disappointed. "They aren't at all alike."

Taking the smaller concho from Jared's hand, Charlotte told him, "I've seen that one before."

"You have? Where?"

"I . . . I don't want to say," she admitted. "He couldn't have had anything to do with it."

"Charlotte . . ."

She sighed. "Billy Wade sometimes wears a vest that's decorated with this same style concho."

Jared's eyebrows shot up. "Billy!" He tugged thoughtfully on his mustache. "Well, I'll be damned."

Chapter 7

JARED MACALESTER WOKE UP EARLY ON THE MORNING OF the sixth of July, still sore from the beating he had taken two nights earlier. As he sat on the edge of the bed, he decided that since there had been no broken bones or any internal injuries, he had no reason to stay under Charlotte Baker's care any longer—no reason, that is, except the desire to do so, for being tended to by Charlotte Baker was a habit he could easily acquire.

It was very quiet in the house, so Jared surmised that Charlotte was still asleep in her bedroom. The only sound was that of the hall clock measuring with its steady tick, just as it had for ninety years, the passage of every second. Charlotte had told him that the clock had belonged to her grandmother and was her proudest possession.

Climbing into his clothes, Jared thought to himself that he did not believe that statement. Oh, he believed that the clock had belonged to her grandmother—but not that it was Charlotte's proudest possession. After seeing the dedication the publisher displayed toward each edition of the *Vindicator,* he was convinced that her proudest possession was the Washington Hand Press she used to get the paper out.

Holding his boots in his hands, Jared opened the bedroom door and tiptoed along the hall to the kitchen. He sat at the kitchen table while he shoved his feet into his boots. Then, as quietly as he could, he built a fire in the cookstove and started a pot of coffee. As he sat waiting for the water to boil, he listened to his stomach rumbling and realized that he was very hungry, having eaten nothing but clear broth the day before. He decided to fix breakfast and set to work making biscuits and frying potatoes and bacon. Within minutes, the entire house was filled with the aroma of his efforts. He had no sooner scrambled the eggs with the potatoes, removed the biscuits and bacon from the oven, and started making the coffee when Charlotte came into the kitchen, dressed in a tailored blue shirtwaist and with her copper-colored hair done up in a neat bun.

Smiling, she asked, "Do you hire out?"

"I have," he answered, clearly surprising her with his reply. "I've worked as a ranch cook." He held a chair out for her, and as she sat, she looked at the food on the table.

"Jared, you continually amaze me," she said as she sat down, her eyes gleaming with pleasure. Spreading a sparkling white napkin on her lap, she declared, "This looks absolutely delicious."

"It is," Jared replied immodestly. "I could still work as a cook at half the ranches in Texas."

"I have no doubt," she laughed. "But, if you don't mind, I would like to make a minor addition to the coffee."

"An addition?"

Opening a small tin box, she took out a sliver of orange peel and held it up for his inspection.

"I discovered this some time ago," she explained as

she lifted the lid of the coffee pot and dropped the orange peel into the brew. "It gives the coffee a nice piquant taste."

When the coffee had steeped long enough for the orange peeling to add its flavor, Charlotte poured each of them a cup, then sat across the table from him, and they began eating.

Jared found himself distracted, for something was nagging at him, a memory way in the back of his mind. But the more he tried to get hold of it, the further away it got. Giving up on trying to grab it, he told her, "I'll be going back to my own room at the hotel today."

"Are you sure you're up to it?"

Gesturing at the food-laden table, he laughed, "Doesn't this prove it? Besides, nothing was broken—and you are a beautiful young widow. People might start asking questions as to why I'm over here."

"Pshaw. Let them ask questions," she rejoined.

"Charlotte, you don't really mean that."

"No," she agreed. "I guess I don't." She looked at him sharply. "What are you going to do now?"

"Since you read my mail, you know why I'm here. And though I may have suffered a blow to my dignity, my mission hasn't changed," Jared reminded her as he poured another cup of coffee. "I'm still trying to find out who's behind the train robberies."

Worry creased Charlotte's forehead as she asked softly, "Jared, why do you do this kind of work?"

Jared was surprised by her question, and it showed on his face. "It's honorable work," he said.

"It's dangerous," she retorted. Pushing back her chair, she stood up and started carrying the dirty dishes over to the sink.

Swiveling in his chair to face her, the Faraday man reminded her, "So is being a railroad engineer or a soldier or a cowboy. There's no such thing as absolute safety. Look at your line of work and what your husband went through. He could have easily been killed."

Sighing, she admitted, "True. But what if . . ." She let the sentence hang.

"What if what?"

"What if you find an answer you don't really want to find? What if your investigation leads you to someone you didn't expect? Someone you care about?"

He considered her words for only a moment before replying, "Charlotte, the person I'm looking for murdered my friend. If my investigation leads me to someone I thought I cared about—then I'll realize that I was mistaken in my judgment about that person."

Still low in the east, the sun sent long bars of light slashing through the tall fir trees, cutting through the morning mist. The high plateau was alive with the sounds of a cattle drive—the bawling of cattle and the shouts and whistles of the wranglers.

Nearly a thousand head of Rocking S cattle milled about in what was a natural pen, an area bordered on the south by a narrow draw and on the north by high mountains. Cowboys darted about on their cutting horses, slowly but inexorably moving the herd eastward.

The moment everyone had been anticipating was here: Ike Stockard was driving the cattle into town. He had already contracted with the railroad to have a special train and cattle cars available—but he had not paid the head tax Josh Wade was demanding, and he had no intention of doing so.

At a meeting held at the Stockard ranch house the night before, the ranchers had decided that Ike would press the issue this morning. However, one of the ranchers had protested vigorously, challenging, "What do you want to do? Start a war?"

He was shouted down by the others, but Ike raised his hand for quiet, then addressed the cautious rancher. "What we want is to be able to raise and deliver our cattle to the market without any interference."

"And you think that's worth fighting over?"

"Oh, yes, it's worth it," Ike said easily.

"How? You tell me how anything is worth maybe getting killed for."

"Were you in the war, Mr. Mitchell?"

"Uh, no. No, I wasn't," the rancher answered.

Gesturing first at himself, then at the assembled crowd, Ike Stockard said, "Well, I was, and so were some of these other men. I wore blue, but some here wore gray. I remember one particularly bitter fight that happened at a little place called Miner's Mill. As battles go, it wasn't a very large one—hell, it probably won't even be mentioned in the history books. But a lot of good men were killed there, good men on both sides, and the funny thing is, we were fightin' over a piece of ground that not one of us had the least damn bit of interest in. The only reason we were fightin' was 'cause General Forrest's boys held it, and we were told to take it." Letting the memory sink in, Ike waited a moment before concluding, "Now, if we were willin' to fight for land that wasn't ours and was never gonna be ours, don't you think we should fight for our own ground?"

Mitchell remained thoughtful for a long moment, then declared that what Ike had said made sense. It was tragic and terrible, but men who had fought in a war for some abstract cause could not be held back from fighting if the cause was right and clear.

Jared Macalester strolled into the restaurant at the Cattlemen's Hotel at midmorning and found Billy Wade having coffee at a table near the front. The young lawman smiled and pushed a chair out with his foot, inviting Jared to join him.

As Millie hurried over with a steaming pot of coffee in her hand, Billy remarked, "Well, it's good to see you up and around again. How're you feeling?"

"Still sore in a few places," Jared groaned in mock despair, "but I'll live."

"I have to confess, you had us a little worried when we carried you over to Charlotte's house night before

last. I'm glad to see that she took good care of you."
Billy smiled. "My brother isn't all that pleased,
though. I think he was about ready to stake his own
claim on the lady, but you beat him to it."

Jared smiled, then he became serious. "I tore this
off Quick during the fight," he said, setting the silver
concho on the table. Placing the other concho up
beside it, he added, "I hoped I'd get a match between
the two, but I didn't."

The deputy looked at Jared curiously, then eyed the
two silver conchos. Setting down his cup, he picked up
the smaller of the two, the one Jared had found at the
site of one of the train robberies. He examined it
closely. "I'll be damned," he finally said. "Where'd
you find this one?"

"Why?"

"Well, it looks like one of mine. I've got a vest
decorated with these."

The Faraday man felt his stomach lurch. "Are you
sure?"

"Not absolutely, 'cause I haven't worn the vest in a
while. But I'd be willing to bet it's missing a concho
and this one will match." He cocked his head and
stared at Jared. "And speaking of which, what did you
mean when you said you were hoping these two'd
match?"

Before Jared could reply, a man appeared in the
door of the restaurant and called excitedly to the
deputy, "Billy! The Stockards is bringin' their cows
in! Josh wants you down to the marshal's office
pronto!"

"Damn!" Billy exclaimed. "I was praying this
wouldn't happen." He stood up and grabbed his hat
from the wall peg, then raced toward the door.

Sighing, Jared scooped the two silver pieces off the
table and dropped them in his pocket. He'd have to
question Billy later. Right now, it seemed a war was
about to be waged—but just maybe he could do
something to prevent it.

* * *

Even before anyone reported the cattle on the move, it had been obvious to Josh Wade that something was afoot when an unscheduled train rolled in, pulling forty empty stock cars, then pulled off the main track and sat there, the empty cars lined up alongside the cattle-loading pens. Forty stock cars holding twenty-five cows per car meant a herd of one thousand head. It was no secret that that was the number of cows the Rocking S Ranch had ready to ship, so simple logic indicated that Ike Stockard was about to bring his cows to town.

But Josh immediately made plans to stop him.

When Jared hurried to the marshal's office to talk to him, Josh was leaning against the front of his desk, shoving shells into the loading slot of his Winchester .30-.30.

"You heard about it?" the lawman asked, his weathered face grim.

"Yes, of course. That's all anyone in town is talking about," Jared replied.

"You can have your choice of weapons," Josh invited, nodding his head toward the gun rack. "Rifle, shotgun, or pistol if you prefer."

"What are you talking about?"

"I'm deputizin' you," Josh explained. "I've already raised a posse to meet the Stockards at the edge of town."

"Wade, you can't be serious!"

"Oh, I'm serious all right," he stated, nodding his head slowly. "I'm very serious. Now, are you for me or against me?"

"Why does it have to be either way? My God, man, there's a full-fledged war brewing here! Is that what you want?"

"It's been comin' on a long time, Jared, you know that. Ike Stockard and I are goin' to go head-to-head and horn-to-horn. One of us is gonna lose, and the other is gonna walk away with control of the whole issue."

Throwing up his hands, the Faraday man shouted,

"One of you? What about the rest of you? If you two go to war, more people than just the Wades and the Stockards will be involved. What about the rest of the town?"

"They can choose sides," Josh retorted flatly.

"Josh, this is crazy! You're the marshal; you're sworn to protect this town. How can you protect them, when there'll be bullets flying all over the place?"

Holding the rifle against his slight paunch, the marshal said stubbornly, "It doesn't have to be that way. All Ike Stockard has to do is obey the law. If he pays the head tax, there won't be any trouble."

Jared grabbed Josh's arm. "Look, you could stop the whole thing if you'd exempt Ike from the head tax."

"Don't you understand, Macalester?" the lawman growled, wrenching his arm free. "If Ike Stockard gets by without payin' the head tax, all the other ranchers will expect to as well. No, it all hinges on Ike Stockard. If I can make him pay, I'll have beaten 'em all."

Staring at the marshal in disbelief, Jared barked, "And that's what this is about? Beating the ranchers?"

"It's about enforcin' the law," Josh snapped. "And until Ironsprings becomes incorporated and someone in legal authority tells me otherwise, the law stands—and it will be enforced. Now, Macalester, if you're gonna be a good citizen and help me enforce this law, get yourself a gun and get into position with the others. If you aren't gonna help, I suggest that you get the hell out of my way and stay off the streets."

Shaking his head, Jared Macalester crossed the room and stepped outside. The sun had risen higher, and the temperature had climbed considerably. Wiping away the sweat from his forehead, Jared thought that there was a noticeable difference in the air aside from just the increased heat, but for a moment or two, he was not sure what it was. Then he realized that the street was nearly deserted. Looking up and down, he saw that even the horses had been removed to avoid being hit by stray bullets. Several of the stores had their shutters closed over their windows, and a man was nailing boards across the front window of the Bitter Drink Saloon. At the west end of town, a couple of wagons had been rolled out into the street and tipped over, forming a barricade, and bales of hay were stacked on either side of the wagons.

Armed men were hurrying into position, confirming that Josh Wade had been successful in raising a fairly sizable posse. Two of the watering troughs were providing cover for possemen, while others were in the loft of the livery and on the roof of the bank. The approach was thoroughly guarded, and there was no way Ike Stockard and his brothers would be able to bring their cattle into town without coming under the guns of the marshal and the men he had assembled.

Disgusted by what was taking place and frustrated by his inability to stop it, Jared Macalester went to the Bitter Drink and shoved his way through the batwings into the relative cool of the saloon. It was deserted except for Katie, the bar girl, and the piano player—who were playing a two-handed game of cards at a table in the back—and Sam, the bartender. Stepping up to the bar, the agent ordered a beer.

"You aren't going to join the posse?" Sam asked, as he set the mug in front of Jared.

"Nope."

"Can't say as I blame you," Sam muttered. "You know, the cowboys are my customers along with the folks here in town. I couldn't start shootin' at them any more'n I could shoot at my next-door neighbor. What I don't understand is how the townfolk got so caught up in it. Why, all of 'em—cowboys and townfolk alike—were all drinkin' together in here just last night."

The batwing doors swung open, and Billy Wade entered. He looked surprised to see Jared.

"Hello, Billy," the agent called. "Did your brother send you after me?"

"Josh? No." He walked to the bar and slapped a

coin down. "Let me have a beer, Sam." Turning to Jared, he sighed. "That damned Ike—with armed men backing him up—is determined to bring his herd into town. And Josh—backed up by *his* armed men—is just as determined to stop him. There doesn't seem to be anybody, anywhere, with any sense." Shaking his head angrily, he grated, "Well, if they're going to fight this war, they're going to do it without me, 'cause I'm not gonna have anything to do with it."

"So you're just going to stay in here out of the way?" Jared asked.

"Can you think of anything better I could do?"

"Talk to Josh. Get him to change his mind."

Billy slammed his hand on the bar so hard that beer splashed out of his mug, and Sam instantly wiped the spill with his bar rag. "Goddammit, man, don't you think I tried?" he replied in an agonized shout. "There's nothing I can do, I tell you! Nothing!"

Jared gulped the rest of his beer, then went to the swinging doors and looked out. Preparations for the battle were just about done. Sighing deeply, he declared, "We can't just stay in here and do nothing."

"Do you have any ideas?" the deputy called from the bar.

Pushing open the doors, Jared said over his shoulder, "No, but maybe Charlotte will." In fact, he was certain that Charlotte would not have the least idea of what to do, but he decided that he wanted to be with her when the fighting started to make sure that she was safe.

"I'll go with you," Billy said, without being invited.

Stepping back outside, the heat hit Jared again like some physical force. He glanced at the thermometer nailed to the porch post and saw that the temperature had climbed to one hundred degrees. Heat waves shimmered in the distance, and as the two men walked to the newspaper office, the street was deathly still, making ordinarily unnoticeable sounds distinct. The sign hanging from the porch in front of the bootmaker's shop squeaked loudly as it swung back and forth in the hot, dry wind, and a piece of tin hummed as the wind whistled through the gap between it and the wall it was patching.

When Jared and Billy reached Charlotte's office, she greeted them nervously. "This is madness," she breathed, closing a large type drawer, then folding her arms across her chest. "We have to stop it somehow."

"Believe me, we've tried," Jared told her. "This thing is happening so fast and getting so big that there's no way we can control it. It's like a runaway freight train or a stam—" Suddenly Jared smiled broadly, and hit his fist into his hand. "A stampede!" he shouted, finishing his sentence. "My God, that's it!" When the others merely looked at him in puzzlement, the agent continued, "Billy, how far out would you say the herd is now?"

Scratching his tawny head, Billy answered, "I'd say about two or three miles."

"That gives us a little more than an hour," Jared quickly calculated. "Charlotte, go down to the loading pens. Make certain there's no water in the troughs— and if there is, get rid of it. Recruit some men to help you, and turn the troughs over if you have to. Just make certain there's no water. Tell them the marshal ordered the water drained."

"Jared, what good is that going to do?" Billy asked.

"The cattle are going to be easily spooked because of the wind and the change in their routine," Jared explained. "And, after the long trek from the ranch, they're going to be thirsty." He paused, and smiled knowingly. "Suppose, just on the edge of town, the cattle began to stampede?"

Billy grinned broadly. "And if there's no water at the depot, they'll run all the way through town to the Ironsprings River."

"That's right," the Faraday man agreed. "Ike and his boys are going to be too busy chasing their herd to start any trouble, and Josh and the posse are going to be too busy trying to get out of the way."

"But a stampede?" Charlotte cut in, "isn't that dangerous for the town?"

"Hell, yes," Jared confirmed. "One thousand cows, trying to squeeze down Front Street are going to do some damage—perhaps a great deal of damage. But the damage is going to be to buildings and things, not to people."

"You think we can get a stampede started?" Billy asked.

Jared snorted. "Believe me, I've seen cattle start stampeding for no reason at all, so yes, I can promise you they will. What I can't promise is that they'll stop at the river. If they're spooked badly enough, they may just keep on running till they drop. If that happens, Ike will have cows spread out all over the territory of Wyoming."

Charlotte looked out the window and sighed. "Let's pray they stop at the river." Then, taking off her ink-covered apron, she dashed to the door and flung it open, declaring forcefully, "Okay, let's get to it."

While Charlotte headed toward the loading pens, Jared and Billy hurried to their horses and mounted up, sneaking out of the north side of town, then riding behind a ridge that put them out of sight of both the defenders of the town and the incoming cowboys. Reaching a spot where they could hide themselves until the herd had passed, they waited.

Finally the herd approached, and the two men drew their revolvers. Jared waited until the herd was halfway passed, and he could tell that they were already nervous, milling to and fro, and clearly thirsty. When Jared and Billy leapt out from behind a low hill and began firing and shouting, the cattle reacted instantly, making a maddened dash straight toward Ironsprings a half mile away.

Marshal Josh Wade was standing at the barricade when one of the men in the posse heard the sounds first.

"Listen, what is that? Thunder?" the man asked.

"I don't see how it could be," Josh replied, looking up. "There isn't a cloud in the sky."

Everyone listened intently as the distant rumble grew louder.

"Look!" someone shouted, pointing to the west. "A cloud of dust! Jeepers, I've never seen such a dust storm!"

"Stampede!" the man standing on the roof of the livery yelled, cupping his hands around his mouth. "Stampede! They're coming right for the town!"

"Sonofabitch!" Josh roared. "Those damn-fool cowboys have stampeded their cattle! They're tryin' to kill us!"

"This barricade ain't gonna stop 'em," the first man shouted, and he and nearly a dozen other men began a mad dash for safety.

The marshal stood mesmerized, watching the herd come nearer and nearer. Although he had faced down many a gunman, he was suddenly petrified with fear and unable to move. The ground was literally trembling with the thunder of four thousand hooves. Josh Wade, the sweat pouring down his face and soaking his shirt collar, was rooted with horror as the herd fast closed the distance between themselves and him.

Suddenly a rider broke ahead of the herd and, spurring his mount hard, leapt the barricade. Reining in in a cloud of dust beside Josh, Ike Stockard offered his stirrup to the marshal. "Wade! Climb on behind me!"

Somehow, Josh found the ability to move then. Placing his foot in the stirrup, he swung up onto the horse behind Ike. The rancher immediately slapped his legs against the side of his horse, and they galloped down the street just a few perilous feet ahead of the mad, rushing herd.

The cattle tore through the barricade as if it were not even there, filling the street from side to side and rampaging in a virtual solid mass. Support pillars were knocked out, and porch roofs caved in; the barber pole was crushed; and hitching rails, watering troughs, and wagons were knocked over and trampled.

The marshal could practically feel the hot breath of the animals on his back, and he was sure he and Ike were going to be run down. Their movement seemed agonizingly slow, and it was as if he were in a nightmare. Then, at the last minute, the rancher saw an open alleyway, and he reined his horse over toward it. Experienced as a cutting horse, the animal made the turn instantly, and they just got out of the street in time to avoid the first steers.

The passing herd created a deafening, trembling roar along with a rolling cloud of dust that completely engulfed the two men. It seemed to continue for an eternity; then, as the last few cattle passed by, the noise receded and the cloud of dust settled. When Ike spurred his horse back onto the main street, Josh saw that the front of the herd had reached the eastern edge of town, heading toward the river. A half-dozen cowboys who had been riding trail chased after the cattle.

Swinging down from Ike's horse, Josh looked up and down Front Street. Three steers were lying in the road, two of them, their necks clearly snapped, were perfectly still. The third was suffering with broken legs, and it was bawling pitifully. The lawman walked over to it, pulled his pistol, and shot it in the head. After a few kicks, it, too, lay still.

Taking off his hat and wiping his sweating forehead, the marshal looked around. The town was a wreck. Not one building had escaped damage. Shingles and smashed boards littered the street, though a closer examination showed that the damage was principally to the boardwalks and porches. The fact that most of the windows had been boarded up in anticipation of the gunfight protected the storefronts from greater damage.

Looking up at Ike, Josh noted wryly, "I guess you won't be shippin' any cows today."

"Or payin' any head tax," Ike added.

"What the hell were you tryin' to do, starting a stampede like that?"

Ike took out a checked bandanna and wiped the dust from his face, then answered, "I was about to ask you the same thing. You started it—or at least you had it started."

"Me?" Josh's eyes narrowed. "What the hell makes you say I had it started?"

Twisting in the saddle, the rancher gestured toward Jared Macalester, who came riding in with Billy. "I saw the trackwalker on the ridge outside of town. He fired his gun and spooked the herd." He glared at the lawman and added, "Everyone knows he's sided up with you, so don't tell me you didn't have somethin' to do with this."

"What?" Josh snapped. He looked over at Jared. "Is he right? Did you start this stampede?"

"Yes," Jared admitted.

"Mister, you're going to jail," Josh said angrily.

"What about me, Josh? Am I going to jail, too?" Billy asked. "'Cause I was with him."

"And I helped, as well," a female voice suddenly put in.

Turning, Josh saw Charlotte Baker standing there, brushing the dust off her dress. He looked from one to the other of them in shock, then shook his head slowly as he stared at the wreckage. "You want to tell me why?" he asked.

"I'll tell you why," Charlotte said. "It was to stop you fools from killing each other."

His eyes narrowing angrily, the marshal told her, "You didn't stop anything, Charlotte . . . you just delayed it." He turned and headed toward his office, though the front of it, like those of many other buildings, was now blocked off by the collapsed overhang of the porch roof. After a few steps, the lawman stopped and looked back toward Ike.

"Stockard?"

"Yeah?"

"Thanks for savin' my life."

"Nothing's changed, Wade. Nothing's changed," Ike declared.

Later that night, when the Bitter Drink was again open for business, Jared Macalester went in and sat at a table in the back of the saloon. While nursing a whiskey, he thought about what Charlotte had asked him: What if his investigation led him where he did not want to go?"

The question had seemed academic then. Now, however, with the possibility that the silver concho he found at the site of the train robbery was Billy Wade's, the question had taken on a whole new meaning.

Was Billy the man behind the money thefts? It could be, since the concho seemed to prove he had been present at at least one of the robbery sites. As a deputy marshal, even in an unincorporated town, he could probably get information as to when money shipments would be transported on the trains. And he could certainly hide behind his badge.

Jared took a swallow of his whiskey, then wiped his mouth with the back of his hand, musing glumly that of all the people he had met since coming to Ironsprings—Charlotte excepted—Billy was the one he liked best.

"Hello, there."

Jared looked up and saw the very man he had been thinking about walking toward his table.

"Started any stampedes lately?" Billy asked with a little laugh.

Jared looked around the saloon. "I don't know as we won many friends by what we did."

"Maybe not. But we saved lives," Billy reminded him. "Say, in all the excitement, you never told me where you found the concho. But I got to thinking about it, and I bet I know where."

"You do? Where?" Jared asked.

Billy smiled broadly. "Why, over at Charlotte Baker's, of course."

"Why would you say that?" Jared asked, feeling his stomach lurch again—only this time even harder, fearing what he was about to hear.

"About two months ago, she asked me if she could borrow my vest—although I never asked her why. I've also never gotten around to getting it back."

It was long past midnight, and Jared lay wide awake in his bed, unable to sleep. His hands folded behind his head, he stared at the shadows on the wall made by the full moon that had risen.

From the moment Billy had told him that he loaned his vest to Charlotte, Jared remembered what it was that had been eluding him way back in his mind—and the memory was making him sick. Charlotte had put a piece of orange peel in the coffee this morning, something Jared had seen only once before. At the site of the last train robbery, where the fifth person had waited with the horses, there were discarded coffee grounds—and in the middle of the discarded grounds was a small piece of orange peel.

Chapter 8

THE WESTBOUND UNION PACIFIC TRAIN SAT IN THE BUS-tling Table Rock station, readying for departure. Walking along the top of the locomotive, the fireman stopped beside the boiler hatch and opened it, then reached for the spout of the water tank, positioning it directly over the hatch. He pulled the spout down, then started in surprise. Instead of the expected torrent, his effort was rewarded with a trickle not much bigger than a man's thumb.

"What the hell?" he blurted, scratching his head and ruffling his thick black hair. Releasing the spout, he made his way back to the rear of the locomotive and yelled down to the engineer, "Abner, there ain't no water in this damn tank!"

"Are you sure, Zeke?" Abner Hodges called up to him, leaning out the window of the cab. The station lights made his bald head gleam like the train's string of highly varnished passenger cars stretched out behind the engine.

Throwing up his hands, the fireman declared, "Well, of course I'm sure! You wanna come up here and see for yourself?"

The engineer then looked down the platform and shouted to the stationmaster who was strutting self-importantly alongside the train, "Meldrum, come here!"

"What is it?" the portly, middle-aged stationmaster asked impatiently as he neared the locomotive. "Can't you see that I'm a busy man?" Then, glaring at the engineer, he added, "And I'll thank you to call me *Mister* Meldrum."

"Well, *Mister* Meldrum, There's no water in the tank," Abner explained.

"Of course there's no water in the tank," the stationmaster replied, as if explaining something that should be obvious. "I received a telegram from the office in Denver telling me to drain the tank to prepare for tomorrow's recaulking of the seams."

The fireman stood at the edge of the engine and stared down at the stationmaster. Squirting a stream of tobacco juice to the ground, very close to where Edward Meldrum was standing, Zeke Jones growled, "I know you and all them brass hats figure out these things. But would you mind tellin' me just how in hell you expect us to make this damn train run without water?"

Sighing and rolling his eyes with exasperation, Meldrum pushed his glasses up on his nose and announced, "When you stopped in Sweetwater, you were supposed to take on enough water to get you through to Ironsprings."

The engineer reached inside the cab, coming back with a fistful of papers. Waving them at the stationmaster, he barked, "If you can show me where in these orders it says we were to do that, I'll eat your damn hat—brass buttons and all."

"You didn't take on water in Sweetwater?"

"Nope." Shaking his head slowly, Abner continued,

"Meldrum, tell me this. Since you know'd we'd be coming through here today, and since the men aren't gonna put the caulking in till tomorrow, why didn't you wait until after we were gone before you drained the tank?"

"My orders were to drain it immediately, to give the tank time to dry out." Frowning, he added defensively, "Besides, I was given to understand that you wouldn't be needing water from our tank."

"Well, you've sure left us in a pickle."

The stationmaster took off his hat and ran his hand through his thinning brown hair. "Well, really," he said, "I have quite enough to do to run my own station. I can't be expected to make all the decisions for the entire railroad, can I?"

Sighing, the engineer looked up and asked the fireman, "Zeke, we got enough water to get to Bitter Creek?"

"I reckon we do."

"All right, close the lid and come on back down. We'll stop at Bitter Creek."

"There's no station there," Meldrum reminded them.

"Don't need a station. All we need is a water tower, and there's one at Bitter Creek for the freights."

Shaking his head, the stationmaster intoned, "Yes, but I can't authorize a stop there."

Abner Hodges stared at the man, his eyes narrowing. "Well, tell me this, *Mister* Meldrum," he began, his voice derisive, "what about when we run out of water? Can you authorize a stop then?" Gesturing at all the passengers boarding the train, he continued, "And what'll I tell all these folks when we do? Sorry, but you'll have to walk the rest of the way?"

Meldrum looked from the engineer to the fireman to the passengers and back again, as if weighing the dilemma. "All right," he finally said. "I'll send word to the other stations down the line that I have authorized a stop at Bitter Creek. But it's for water only, do you understand?" Putting his cap back on, he then hurried away to the telegraph office.

Six miles west of Table Rock, four horsemen waited under the looming dark shadow of a solitary water tower, which was all that marked this stop on the railroad maps. The town of Bitter Creek itself was a fly-blown little place about five miles south of the track, and the water tower had been put in to take advantage of the creek that gave the town its name.

Although the place was deserted, a cacophony of insect noise filled the night. There was a particularly bad infestation of mosquitoes, and the riders battled them as they waited.

"What if it don't stop?" Logan asked, slapping at one mosquito, then scratching the places where others had bitten.

"It'll stop," Tim Quick assured his three cohorts. "There's no water in Table Rock, so if they don't stop at this tank, they won't even make it to Ironsprings." Turning to one of his men, he ordered, "Tucker, climb up on top of the tank and see if you can see the train."

Obeying orders, Tucker balanced himself carefully and stood on the saddle of his horse, then pulled himself up onto the ladder and started climbing to the top. When he had reached his goal, he shouted down, "Don't see it yet." He paused, then asked, "Say, Tim, how much money is this train carryin', anyway?"

"Fifteen hundred dollars," Quick answered. "But seven hundred fifty goes to the person that set it up."

"When are you gonna tell us who that is, Tim?" Logan asked.

Quick whirled and glared at him. "What do you want to know for?"

"Well, I was just thinkin'," Logan said, a frown on his thin, craggy face, "that if somethin' happened to you on one of these jobs—I mean, it could, you know, and if it did, we wouldn't know who to give the share to . . . or who to have set up the next job."

Quick snorted. "You're just gonna have to hope nothin' happens to me, ain't ya?" Then he laughed. "I'll tell you this. You'd be surprised if you knew who it was."

"Hey, boys!" Tucker suddenly called. "I see it comin'!"

"All right, Tucker," Quick directed, "stay up there, and you and Logan'll cover the fireman and engineer. Me and Grub'll take care of the mail car." The other three slid from their saddles, ground tying the four mounts, and waited expectantly.

"Get ready!" Quick hissed at the sound of the train's brakes being applied, and each of them pulled a kerchief up over the lower half of his face.

Minutes later, the train squealed and ground to a halt with the engine directly under the water tank. The fireman came out of the cab, climbed up onto the top of the locomotive, walking quickly to the boiler and raising the lid. Pulling the tank's spout down, Zeke then jerked on the rope, and water started cascading into the nearly empty chamber in a loud gush.

So intently was the crewman watching the water that he did not see Tucker dropping down from the tank behind him. When the gunman suddenly poked his gun into Zeke's ribs, he jumped with fright.

"What the hell? Mister, what are you doing out here?" Zeke asked, clearly so startled that he was unaware of what was happening.

Tucker laughed. "Hell, don't you know? We're robbin' this here train."

At the same time, Logan, his gun already cocked, climbed up into the cab and pointed the weapon at the engineer. "Get 'em up, mister," he demanded, and Abner Jones threw up his hands obligingly.

With the fireman and engineer under control, Quick and Grub walked down to the mail car, and Quick banged on the door.

"What is it?" a muffled voice called from inside.

"Open up!"

"You know we ain't supposed to open the door between stops."

"Open up!" Quick repeated gruffly.

"All right," the mail clerk responded hesitantly as he slowly slid back the door, "but if I get in trouble, I want it understood that you—" At the sight of the two masked men holding guns pointed at him, the young man broke off his words and stepped back, throwing his hands in the air. "Damn! You ain't the conductor."

"We sure ain't," Quick chortled.

Hearing the sound of footsteps crunching on the gravel along the tracks, Quick turned. The conductor was walking toward the front of the train, and when he got close enough to see what was happening, he stopped, then turned and started running back toward the rear of the train.

"Hold up!" he started shouting. "The train's being robbed!"

"Stop right there, you!" Quick yelled, aiming his gun at the fleeing man. When the conductor did not obey, Quick fired, hitting him in the back of the head. The man screamed once as he fell, sprawling facedown on the gravel.

A woman from inside the train shrieked, and a man stuck his head out to see what was going on.

"Get back in there!" Quick ordered, then fired. His bullet chipped away the varnished mahogany window frame so close to the passenger's face that it sent a spray of splinters into the man's cheek.

While commotion reigned inside the passenger cars, Quick turned his attention back to the baggage clerk. "Now," he snapped, "give me the money."

"What money? We're not carrying any money."

Quick pulled the hammer back on his revolver and aimed it at the clerk's head. "I just killed your conductor," he warned. "You think I'd worry any about killin' you? Now, you got one thousand and five hundred dollars in a bag headed for the bank in Green

River, and I aim to get it from you one way or another."

The platform alongside the depot at Ironsprings was crowded, filled not only with those who would normally meet the night train, but with the curious who had heard the series of short whistles as the train approached the station that announced something was wrong. Among those who had heard the signal were Jared Macalester and Billy Wade, and while they waited for the train to crawl to a stop, the Faraday man remarked, "I have a feeling I know what that something wrong is."

Nodding, the deputy muttered, "Yeah, me, too."

Their fears were confirmed even before the train had fully stopped when the engineer shouted, "We were robbed, and the conductor was killed!"

Since Josh Wade was away on personal business, the interrogation of the crew and passengers was undertaken by Billy. Although Jared would have liked to interview the witnesses directly, it would not be possible without giving away his identity. However, he did stand by as Billy spoke with the witnesses, interjecting certain thoughts of his own.

Finally, when all the questions had been asked and the train with a new conductor was sent on its way nearly three hours behind schedule, Jared offered, "Buy you a drink, Billy?"

"Yeah," the lawman agreed, "might as well. I'm not going to learn anything else standing around down here." He then shrugged and added, "Not that I can do anything with what I've learned, anyway. Damn! It's so frustrating, not having any authority outside of Ironsprings."

As the two men walked from the depot to the Bitter Drink Saloon, evidence of the rebuilding of the stampede-destroyed town was visible all around them. Although the carpenters had stopped work for the night, piles of freshly cut lumber and newly split shingles were stacked in the street in front of the stores. In a compromise worked out by the Administration Committee, the Stockards were exempted from having to pay the head tax when their cattle were finally loaded onto the special train and shipped, but in return, Ike had agreed to pay for all the repair and reconstruction of the town.

When the two men stepped inside the Bitter Drink —one of the first buildings to be repaired—they sensed the air of excitement caused by the news of the train robbery. Jared Macalester knew that it was not that the people were happy the railroad had been robbed, it was just a change in their routine and, as such, an exciting event.

He heard someone repeating the story that was already all over town. "They say that whoever held up that train put a bullet in the back of the conductor's head from over a hundred feet! And that's in the dark at a moving target!"

Jared and Billy got their beers and found a table, and as they sat, the deputy's blue eyes seemed to darken as he grumbled, "What we don't need is for folks to start making heroes out of these damn train robbers."

Watching Billy's face closely, Jared asked, "Do you have any idea who they might be?"

"Nope, not a one." Billy took a swallow of his beer, then set the mug down. "But like I said, it wouldn't matter if I did, since I couldn't do anything about it."

"There's that old jurisdiction again."

"Yep."

Trying to keep his voice light and curious rather than intently interested, the Faraday man commented, "I understand. Still, it might be interesting to try and figure out who it was—and who planned it."

"What do you mean, who planned it? The ones who did it planned it."

"Maybe," Jared said, taking off his Stetson. "But in every previous robbery, there's been evidence that there was someone else involved, a fifth party who's never been seen."

Billy looked at Jared suspiciously. "How do you know all this?"

Shrugging, Jared pointed out, "I work for the railroad, remember? I've seen all the reports."

"Oh, right." The deputy's face was thoughtful for a moment, then he said, "Well, I sure as hell didn't know about a fifth person. I'll be damned."

Picking up his mug, Jared looked at Billy over the rim and asked, "Do you remember the silver concho I found? The one you said is yours?"

"Yes, of course."

"Would you like to know where I found it?"

"I know where you found it." Billy grinned, looking like a mischievous boy. "You found it over at Charlotte's place."

Jared took a swig of his beer, then responded, "No, I found it at the site of one of the train robberies."

The deputy's eyebrows shot up. "What? What the hell was it doing out there? Come to think of it, what were *you* doing out there?"

"I'm a trackwalker, remember?"

"Oh, yeah."

"How did it get there, Billy?"

Shrugging, the deputy answered, "Damned if I know. I didn't even know it was . . . Wait a minute." Billy's blue eyes narrowed in anger. "Macalester, I'm not sure I like the way this little talk of ours is going," he growled. "Are you accusing me of being one of the train robbers?"

Putting up his hands in protest, Jared retorted, "I'm not accusing anyone of anything. I just made the observation that I found your silver concho at the site of one of the train robberies, and I wondered how it got there."

"Well I didn't drop it there," Billy snapped. He looked around to make sure no one was listening, then whispered harshly, "And what's more, I don't believe Charlotte Baker dropped it there, either."

The familiar sick feeling in his stomach returned, but Jared did his best to ignore it. Putting a placating hand on Billy's shoulder, he told him, "Look, I didn't intend to make you angry. My God, how do you think I feel? So far everything I've found points right at Charlotte Baker . . . a woman I might very well be in love with."

Billy sighed and stroked his chin. "All right," he mused, "what if it is her? You aren't a lawman, so you can let it drop."

The Faraday man was on the verge of revealing his true identity to the deputy, but he checked himself. "I wish I could," Jared admitted, "but I have to know."

Pushing his hat back on his head, Billy stared at his companion and asked, "Jared, why on earth would you want to prove the guilt of a fine woman like Charlotte Baker?"

"If she's guilty, then she's an accomplice in at least two murders," Jared pointed out. "That wouldn't make her such a fine woman, would it?"

"No," Billy agreed, "I guess not."

Finishing up his beer, Jared set the mug down on the table and looked around the crowded, noisy saloon. He then turned back to Billy and observed, "If she *is* guilty, there's no doubt that every single person in this room would get the surprise of his life."

Early the next morning Jared Macalester stood at the window of his second floor room, looking down on Front Street. In the early-morning sunlight, the newly painted buildings took on a golden glow, and the town was actually very very pretty. One of the glowing buildings was the newspaper office, which Jared studied for a long moment.

After climbing into bed the night before, he had lain awake for hours, weighing the evidence and asking himself over and over was Charlotte Baker mixed up in the train robberies? Surely not, he had finally concluded. The agent was generally a very good judge of character, and nothing about Charlotte's character pointed to her guilt. That is—he now admitted in the cold light of day—unless he was allowing his judgment to be colored by his feelings. Was that possible? Did he care so much for her that he was willing to turn a blind eye to evidence?

Now more than ever what she had suggested about his investigation leading him to someone he did not want to be guilty came back to haunt him. Was she talking about herself? Was she, even then, sowing seeds of doubt to cause him to go through just what he was going through at this moment?

With an anguished sigh, he forced himself to look away from the newspaper building, and in so doing he caught sight of Josh Wade going into the telegraph office by the depot. Jared smiled to himself. Whether the townspeople were for their marshal or against him, they would have to admit that he was a hard worker. In fact, the Faraday man had never seen a peace officer work harder.

When Josh stepped inside the telegraph office, he walked over to the counter and filled out a form, then handed it to the telegrapher.

"Send this out immediately, will you, Carl?" the lawman requested.

The old man smiled. "Sure thing, Marshal. I'll—" Suddenly the key started clacking with the call letters for Ironsprings, alerting Carl Masters to an incoming message. "I guess it'll have to wait till this one's done," the telegrapher told the lawman.

"Mind if I help myself to a cup of coffee, Carl?" Josh asked.

"Go ahead," the telegrapher replied, starting for the table where the telegraph key was clicking away. Putting his hand on the key, he sent the message that Ironsprings was standing by, and then the message started coming in:

TO JARED MACALESTER. IT WAS A SUNNY DAY ON THE 7TH STOP IT MAY RAIN BY THE 10TH STOP LOOK FOR A CHANGE

IN THE WEATHER IN CHEYENNE STOP
UNCLE MATT

"Well, now, if that ain't a hell of a note," Carl chuckled as he finished writing down the message. "Some darn fool just spent eighty cents to send a weather report."

When Jared received the telegram later that morning, noting that Matthew Faraday—Uncle Matt— had sent it, he immediately decoded it. When included in sentences dealing with the weather, numbers were to be added together. Seven and ten was seventeen, which meant his assistance was needed for something that was going to take place on the seventeenth of this month. To find out what was going to happen, Jared was instructed to go Cheyenne, and the "change" meant another Faraday agent would be there to give him further information. Since Faraday would be making allowances for the fact that eastbound trains to Cheyenne arrived on even-numbered days, Jared would be expected to meet the agent there on the sixteenth in preparation for the following day's events.

It was barely six o'clock, but already the Bitter Drink Saloon bustled with activity and raucous voices. A loud peal of laughter rang from the table nearest the piano, where three men and three women seemed to be having a very good time.

"Hey, piano player, play us some music," Grub, one of the customers at the table, shouted.

"Well, give him some money, Grub," Tucker laughed, hugging the bar girl on his lap. "You don't expect him to play for nothin', do you?"

"Yeah, don't forget, it cost him somethin' for piano lessons," Logan added. Turning his attention to the woman sitting beside him, he kissed her soundly.

"Piano lessons," Grub echoed dully. Giggling, he

pushed the woman off his lap, then got up and walked over to the piano. He shoved a dollar into the glass sitting on the edge, then instructed, "Now, play me a tune."

"Thank you, sir," the piano player responded with a broad smile. "What would you like to hear?"

"'Buffalo Gals,'" Grub snickered. He returned to the table, then pulled the waiting bar girl back down on his knee. "'Buffalo Gals,'" he said again, "'cause I got me one of my own, right here." He squeezed the girl, and she laughed provocatively, putting down her glass on the table that was littered with empty bottles.

"'Buffalo gals, won't you come out tonight, come out tonight, come out tonight,'" the six at the table began singing, loudly and out of tune. Continuing to grind out the music, the piano player smiled a long-suffering smile, for his ear had long ago been deadened by such off-key renditions.

From his table, Jared Macalester looked over at the revelers and remarked to his companion, "It's a little unusual to see those boys in here, isn't it, Billy? I thought they spent most of their time down at the Bucket of Blood."

"Yeah, they do," Billy replied. "But since they got a hold of some money, they started coming here."

"Where do you think they got all the cash they've been throwing around?" Jared asked.

Leaning back in his chair, the deputy stared at Tucker and the others. "That's a damned good question," Billy finally muttered. "Where *did* they get it?" He was silent for another long moment, then turned to the Faraday agent and said, "You know, Adam was working on this train robbery business the night he was shot. He told me he got an idea while he was at Sweetwater. As it turns out, the train that was last robbed was supposed to stop at Sweetwater to fill the tank, but it didn't. If it *had* taken on water there, it wouldn't have had to stop at Bitter Creek, and the robbers wouldn't have been waiting there to rob it."

Jared looked at him sharply. "What are you getting at?"

"Maybe he saw those boys there. Could be, you know. They sure didn't start spending all this money until after the robbery. How much money was taken from the train?"

"Fifteen hundred dollars."

"Fifteen hundred dollars, eh?" The deputy looked back at the other table and mused, "I wonder how much they've spent in here tonight." He glanced at Jared, his eyebrows arching. "Let's figure it up. Okay, they've got four bottles of whiskey at a dollar and a quarter a bottle . . . that's five dollars."

"And they've bought a couple of rounds for everyone in the place," Jared reminded him.

"All right, that's about ten more dollars. The girls . . . um, three dollars each, that's nine. Then last night they probably spent around fifteen dollars at the Pleasure Palace, making it thirty-nine dollars. Let's add another ten . . . no, make it eleven, just so it'll come out even." He paused, then said, "All totaled, they've been on a fifty-dollar spending spree. Now, if they robbed that train, they should have more than fourteen hundred dollars left."

Jared realized there was another factor missing from their equation. "What about Quick?" he reminded Billy.

"Yeah, you're right. These boys and Tim Quick are joined at the hip—and there *were* four men involved. Okay, we'll say Quick was with them, meaning if they robbed the train and took equal shares, how much should they have left? Remembering that they've already spent fifty dollars?"

Jared figured it out. "Between them, they should have a little over a thousand dollars," he estimated.

Billy stood up.

"What are you going to do?"

"Find out how much money they have by searching them," he said simply.

The agent thought Billy was about to act imprudently. Shaking his head, he pointed out, "You don't have the authority to do anything like that."

"The hell I don't," Billy retorted, picking up his shotgun. "This is all the authority I need." He walked over to the table and stood beside it, cradling the shotgun in his arms. One of the threesome offered Billy a drink, but the lawman ignored the invitation and demanded that they all stand and empty their pockets onto the table top.

"Hold on, Deputy, you don't have no right to—" Before Logan could finish his statement, Billy backhanded the barrel of his gun across Logan's face, knocking the man to the floor with a bleeding lip. The girl who had been sitting beside him jumped away, and the other two bar girls leapt off the laps they had been sitting on and fled to safety.

Glaring at each of the three men in turn, Billy roared, "I said put all your money on the table! Now!"

Tucker helped Logan up, then the men began emptying their pockets as ordered. Within a few moments, a pile of wadded-up greenbacks and coins stood in the middle of the table.

"Deputy, are you . . . are you *robbin'* us?" Logan asked.

Ignoring Logan's question, Billy called, "Jared, get over here and count this money."

The Faraday agent ambled over and started counting, finally coming up with a total of four hundred thirty-eight dollars and sixty-two cents.

"Where'd you get this money?" Billy demanded.

"We won it playing poker," Tucker answered.

"You mean all of you suddenly got lucky at the same time?"

Simultaneously, Tucker answered yes, while Logan contended it had just been one of them.

"Well, which is it?"

Tucker and Logan looked at each other, then Logan cleared his throat and explained, "See, I was the one who actually won, but since the others put up the money for me to play with, we figure we all won. That's why you could say that all of us got lucky."

Looking at the man skeptically, Billy signaled to Jared, and each of them grabbed one of Logan's arms and led him out of earshot from the others. Billy then asked what his winning hand had been. Releasing Logan, he then called each of the others over and repeated the question—getting a different response each time.

Walking back to the table, Billy growled, "Seems like none of you fellas was watching the same game being played."

"Deputy, I was the one playing, so that's why they don't know," Logan insisted.

"Where'd you hide the rest of the money?"

The threesome looked innocently at each other. "What rest of the money? This is all there is," Logan insisted.

Billy looked at them for a moment, then, with an impatient wave of his hand, dismissed them and went back to his own table. After he and Jared sat back down, Billy picked up his drink and stared at the glass. "They're lying about the card game, but it doesn't seem like they have enough money to be involved with the train robbery."

"Maybe they hid it somewhere," Jared suggested.

"I don't think so. In the first place, those stupid bastards wouldn't have enough sense to remember where they hid it. And in the second place, the only thing I believe of what they told me is that that's all the money there is.

Jared thought a moment, then suggested, "Maybe Quick's cut was bigger than we supposed."

But Billy disagreed with that idea. Sighing, he allowed, "I guess I was wrong. I guess they didn't have anything to do with it after all."

Looking over at the cowboys, Jared shook his head. "Maybe not. But the money had to come from somewhere, and I don't believe for a minute that they won it in a card game." He thought over the threesome's responses for a few moments, then decided he had had enough of their boisterous noise. He looked at the big clock over the end of the bar and announced to Billy, "Well, I think I'll stop by and see Charlotte." He then stood and put on his hat. "If I see you later tonight, I'll buy you a beer before I turn in."

"Sound's like a sensible thing to do," Billy laughed, raising his glass to Jared.

Jared threaded his way across the smoky saloon and pushed his way out the batwing doors. Breathing deeply of the fresh air, he turned and headed down Front Street. Reaching the *Vindicator* office a few minutes later, he knocked on the window to alert Charlotte of his presence, then went inside. As she came toward him, he was surprised to see her wiping tears from her eyes.

"Charlotte, what is it?"

"It's my sister," she told him. "I've just received a telegram. Her little girl is seriously ill, and she's asked me to come to Denver. I know I have a lot of work to do here, but I feel that I must go. She needs me."

"Of course you must go," Jared commiserated.

"Johnny can put out the paper for me while I'm gone. You will tell everyone, won't you, that I'll be back as soon as I can?"

"Of course. And don't worry," Jared assured her lightly, "the town will still be here when you get back."

She looked up at him, staring deep into his eyes. "Will *you?*" After a moment of silence, Charlotte let out a long, audible sigh. "There," she breathed, "I've said it. It's you I hate leaving as much as the town. I just couldn't bear it if I got back and you were gone . . . left without even so much as a farewell."

Jared smiled and gently touched each of her tear tracks. "I'll still be here when you get back," he promised.

"Good. In that case you can see me off at the depot

tomorrow morning. Meet me at my house, if you will."

"You can count on it."

As the train pulled out, Jared stood on the platform and waved at the redhead. Then he turned and started walking back to the center of town, thinking that this was the opportunity he had been looking for to do some further investigating about Charlotte Baker. He prayed that if he found anything concrete, it would establish her innocence—not her guilt.

Chapter 9

JARED MACALESTER DECIDED TO WAIT UNTIL THE FOLLOWing day before going to both Charlotte Baker's house and her office to look around. Beginning early in the afternoon, he stood at his hotel room window, watching the newspaper office. Finally at about two o'clock his patience was rewarded, and he saw Johnny Rogers step out of the newspaper office with a bundle of papers under his arm, then turn and lock the door behind him. He headed up Front Street and began making his deliveries.

Johnny paused and handed a paper to Josh Wade, who took it and continued his way slowly down the street reading the paper, looking up occasionally to exchange greetings with passersby. The marshal seemed to be heading for the railroad depot, and Jared watched until he was out of sight. It certainly would not do for Josh to catch him snooping around in a closed newspaper office.

Hurrying out of his room and down the stairs, Jared walked casually to the newspaper office, then slipped around back to the rear entrance. The agent was surprised at how easy it was to get in and hoped that Charlotte did not keep much of value there. As he looked around the office, he realized that he had no idea of what he was actually looking for, but he assumed that if he saw something important, it would make an impression on him.

Starting first with the file of newspapers, he found the ones that carried the stories about the train robberies and saw that in each case Charlotte had come out with the strongest possible denouncement of them. Sighing, Jared thought that it did not really mean much. If she was involved in them in any way, denouncing them would be the perfect smokescreen to throw suspicion away from herself. He looked around a while longer; then, finding nothing else in the newspaper office that was significant, he went to her house.

Once more going around to the back, he again easily gained entry through a window. He walked down the hallway of the two-story dwelling to the parlor, and as he stood there, smelling the distinctive smells he had learned to associate with Charlotte—lavender soap, a hint of her perfume—he felt as if he were somehow violating her. The feeling was so strong that he almost turned and left, but then he decided he was committed now. He had gone this far, and he had to go on with it because he had to know definitively if she were a part of the robberies or not.

When he stepped into the room, the first thing he noticed was a photograph on the small mahogany desk in the corner of the room. Picking up the frame, Jared presumed that the man in the photograph was her late husband. He was pleasant looking though not particularly handsome, and he stared out with deep, intense eyes over a bushy handlebar mustache. It was obvious that Cap had been quite a bit older than Charlotte.

Crossing over to the closet, he opened it and riffled through it. Leaning against the back, he found a rolled-up poster, and when he took it out and unrolled it, it turned out to be a showbill of a young woman in a fringed buckskin dress. She had a smoking pistol in each hand, and the legend read:

CHARLOTTE AMES
World's greatest female pistoleer
Performing with Dr. Benteen's Wonderful
Medicine Show

Though it was an artist's rendering, not a photograph, there was no doubt in Jared's mind that the picture of the sharpshooter was Charlotte Baker.

The Faraday man then went back to the desk and examined its contents. In one of the drawers he found a small notebook, which turned out to be a record of bank deposits—and four sizable ones had recently been made. Though there was not an exact correspondence between the dates of deposit and the dates of the train robberies, with a sinking heart he realized that in each case the deposit had been made shortly after the robbery, and all deposits were in amounts commensurate with what might have been a share of the money taken.

His heart pounding, Jared put the account book back in the drawer, then shut it. He walked back through the house, making certain he had not left any sign of his entry, then let himself out the back door and hurried away.

As he headed back to his hotel room, he thought to himself that he had never felt more miserable about anything in his life.

It was early evening when Jared Macalester made his way to the telegraph office at the depot. He needed to send a telegram to Matthew Faraday, confirming that he would—as instructed—be in Cheyenne on July sixteenth, one week hence. Stepping into the depot, he found Josh Wade leaning on the counter, talking with the telegrapher.

"Evening, Marshal," the agent said. "How are you?"

"Just fine, Jared, just fine," the marshal answered. "What are you doin' down here?"

"Well, my uncle needs me to be in Cheyenne on the sixteenth," Jared explained, "and I came to send a telegram telling him I'll be coming."

"Family matter?"

Tugging at his mustache, Jared acknowledged, "Yeah, you might say that." He then smiled at the telegraph clerk and had just started talking to him when the telegraph key began clicking. Carl Masters told him he would have to wait until the wire was clear to send the message.

Jared turned and gazed out the window, seemingly biding his time and disinterested in the series of dots and dashes. In fact, all Faraday agents had been schooled in Morse code, and he was as fast—if not faster—than most telegraphers. Listening carefully to the message that was being received, it stated that sixty thousand dollars was being sent from Cheyenne on the seventeenth of July. *I wouldn't be at all surprised*, he said to himself, *if that's why I've been ordered by Matthew Faraday to meet with someone from the agency in Cheyenne.*

He was suddenly aware that someone was standing directly beside him, and he turned and found Josh looking at him curiously. "When did you say you had to be in Cheyenne?" the lawman asked.

"On the sixteenth," Jared replied.

"Well, I hope you have a pleasant trip." Smiling, he added, "'Course, I'll probably see you again before you go."

Laughing, Jared agreed, "More than likely, since we seem to eat and drink in the same places."

The marshal nodded good-bye to Carl, then left the depot, heading toward his office.

"Now, sir," the telegrapher said to Jared, "let's get that message of yours sent."

* * *

As Jared walked back to his hotel, he passed the newspaper office and felt a twinge of conscience. He should not have broken into Charlotte's house and place of business; he had no right to do that. And the more he thought about it, the more he was convinced that she had nothing to do with the robberies. After all, he had worked for Faraday for quite some time now, and he had solved a number of cases with nothing stronger to go on than a feeling in his gut. That feeling had yet to steer him wrong, and the feeling he had now—despite any evidence to the contrary—was that Charlotte Baker was innocent.

Having come to that conclusion, the Faraday man squared his shoulders, feeling as if a great weight had been lifted from them. Trying to find the evidence against Charlotte had already taken too much time and, he believed, had not advanced the case. He would just keep on until he discovered who the guilty party was. Proving the guilt of another would establish the innocence of Charlotte, and that was just what he intended to do.

The following week Jared Macalester sat having a drink with the two Wade brothers in the Bitter Drink Saloon. It was nearing ten o'clock when the agent declared he had to leave, needing to get up early the following morning. "I've got a few hours' worth of track to check before I catch the train to Cheyenne—which means I'd better catch some winks, as well."

Billy Wade watched Jared leave, then, a frown creasing his handsome face, asked, "Tell me, does it seem to you like he's been acting peculiar ever since Charlotte Baker left?"

Josh snorted and twirled his gray mustache. "Well, maybe he's just a lovesick puppy."

"No, I'm afraid it's more than that," the deputy responded solemnly. "I'm afraid Jared thinks Charlotte is the one he's been looking for."

The marshal stared at his brother, clearly dumbfounded. "Lookin' for? Lookin' for, for what?"

"The train robberies," Billy replied.

Josh's eyes grew wider. "What?"

Sighing, the deputy lowered his voice and repeated, "The train robberies. I think he may actually believe Charlotte is behind them." He then explained how Jared had found a silver concho at one of the robbery sites—which belonged to a vest he had loaned the publisher.

Josh Wade leaned closer to his brother, asking, "Billy, do you know somethin' I don't know? Like, why the hell Jared Macalester was pokin' around at one of the robbery sites in the first place?"

"Yeah," Billy admitted, "I guess I do know something you don't know." He looked around to make sure no one could hear him, then whispered, "Jared Macalester is a Faraday man."

"A Faraday man!" Josh exclaimed hoarsely. "I knew it! I knew it had to be somethin' like that. I didn't know what it was, but I knew he wasn't a trackwalker." He looked at Billy questioningly. "How did you find out?"

"I found out from Charlotte. She told me just before she left for Denver because she wanted me to keep an eye on him—to keep him from getting into any trouble."

Suddenly Josh began laughing.

"What is it?" Billy asked, narrowing his blue eyes in bewilderment. "What's so funny?"

"Jared Macalester," Josh said. "Here he's told only one person in this whole town who he is, and now he's suspectin' her of the very thing he's investigatin'."

Billy shook his head, muttering, "I guess I don't see much humor in the situation." He then added, "I'm going to tell him we know about him."

"No, don't do that," Josh responded quickly.

"Why not? If he knew she was concerned enough about him to worry about him, it would probably convince him that she's not guilty."

Josh leaned back in his chair and folded his arms across his paunch. "On the other hand, it might make even more trouble for her if he knew she told us," he pointed out. "I mean it, Billy, don't say a word about this."

"All right," Billy agreed, shrugging.

The two men finished their drinks, then stood up and crossed the saloon, pushing out the swinging doors. Billy started walking toward the jail when the marshal abruptly stopped him with a hand on his shoulder.

"I'll see you later, Billy."

"Where you going? Aren't you going to make your rounds?"

"Later. Right now, I'm goin' over to the Pleasure Palace. I've got some business to take care of." He grinned salaciously. "Some personal business."

"Josh, I wish you'd sell that place."

"Are you crazy, little brother? The Pleasure Palace makes more money than any other business operation I'm runnin' around here." He snickered, "And besides, I get all them—what do you call 'em? Oh, yeah, perquisites."

"Yeah, well, I wish you would sell it and the other businesses, too. Or else . . ." he let the sentence hang.

"Or else what?"

"Or else quit being a marshal," Billy mumbled. "It doesn't seem right to me. Something like that can get into the way of a lawman's responsibility."

Josh laughed heartily and clapped his brother's back. "Well, that's the difference between you and me, Billy. You look at being a lawman as a responsibility. I look at it as an opportunity."

Chapter 10

THE SOUND OF A PISTOL SHOT ROLLED DOWN THE MOUNtainside, then echoed back from the neighboring mountains. Holding a smoking pistol and turning to his audience of three, Tim Quick smiled broadly, pleased at having broken a thrown whiskey bottle with his marksmanship.

"I'd like to see Macalester do that," the gunman boasted with a toss of his blond head.

"Tim, why do you worry so much about Macalester? He ain't nothin' but a trackwalker," Grub commented.

Quick poked the empty shell casings out of the cylinder of his pistol and began shoving in new cartridges. Looking at Grub with disdain, he mocked, "And you ain't nothin' but an idiot. You think someone who can shoot like him is just a trackwalker?"

"Well, then, what is he? I mean if he ain't just a trackwalker."

"He's a Faraday man," Quick snapped. He nodded at Tucker, who threw up another bottle. Following the bottle to the top of its arc, Quick then fired just before the bottle started back down and his bullet shattered it.

"How'd you find that out, Tim?" Logan asked.

"I got ways of findin' out things like this," Quick replied mysteriously. He then holstered his revolver and ordered, "Throw up two bottles this time."

Obliging him, Tucker tossed one bottle into the air, and Grub tossed the other. Quick then drew and fired twice, hitting them both.

"Whoooeee, Tim, that was some kind of shootin'!" Grub exclaimed. "That was even better'n when you shot the conductor in the back of the head."

"Yeah, that was a good shot, wasn't it? It bein' night-time, and him runnin' away from me and all." He smirked, "The next conductor we run into's gonna be our last."

Tucker cocked his head and stared at the gunman. "What do you mean? What do you got in mind?"

"We're about to rob us another train," Quick explained, "but it's gonna be carryin' more money than all the other jobs we ever did put together." He twirled the pistols on his fingers a couple of times, then put them back in the holsters.

"How much money?" Tucker asked.

Pausing until he had their complete attention, he smiled slowly and announced, "Sixty thousand dollars."

"Sixty thousand dollars? That's more money than there is in all of Wyomin'," Tucker breathed. "Who's ever seen so much money?"

"We're goin' to," Quick chortled. "We ain't only gonna see it . . . we're gonna take it."

Stroking his scruffy beard, Logan observed, "Even givin' half of it away to our 'friend' will still leave a lot for us."

Quick shook his head. "It would—but our friend ain't gettin' half of it this time. I'm keepin' half for myself, and you boys can divide the other half amongst you."

"Whooeee! You mean we're keepin' it all?" Grub crowed.

Logan interjected, "Hold on, there's a problem with that. Tim, you know who this fella is, we don't, so after we pull this doublecross, you know who to look out for. We won't have any idea."

Shrugging, Quick suggested, "Then I reckon you're just gonna have to be extra careful."

After looking thoughtful for a long moment, Logan finally said, "All right, but if we're gonna do this, it ought to be worth the extra risk to us. Why not be fair about it, and let's divide the take equally?"

"You don't like me takin' half the money, is that it?" Quick asked.

Logan looked at the other two men, and their eyes reflected their support. "No, we don't," Logan answered. "We ain't said nothin' before 'cause there was someone else takin' a share, too—someone we never saw. But since there ain't no one else this time, we figure it's about time you played it straight with us."

In the blink of an eye, a gun was in Quick's right hand and pointed at Logan. Smiling evilly, the gunslinger queried, "You think these boys deserve a bigger share, do you?"

Logan's face had paled, and he held up his hands in supplication. "Tim . . . Tim, what are you doin'?" He took a step backward. "Listen, Tim, I didn't mean nothin' by it. I was just jawin', that's all."

"Oh, I think you're right," Quick snarled. "I think they should get a bigger share."

"Tim, no!"

Pulling the trigger, the gun roared and bucked in Quick's hand, and a split second later, a hole appeared in Logan's forehead. The impact of the slug knocked him down onto the rocks, where he lay still with his eyes glazed and his mouth open from its last cry of terror.

"Well, boys," Quick said, giggling as if he had just pulled off a very funny joke, "I guess Logan had a point there. You two should have more money—so now you can divide what would have been his share." The gunman looked at Grub and Tucker, who were staring in disbelief at the body of their friend. "That is, unless maybe you think your share ain't gonna be big enough."

"No, no," Tucker blurted. "It sounds plenty big enough to me."

"Yeah, he wasn't speakin' for us, Tim," Grub insisted.

"I thought you boys might see it my way," Quick retorted. Motioning them over, he then explained, "Now, we got us a little plannin' to do. We ain't stealin' no fifteen hundred dollars this time, so I figure the job is going to be a bit harder. You're gonna have to pay attention, and do everything just the way I say."

The railroad station in Cheyenne was bustling with activity when Jared Macalester, attired in a brown suit that gave the impression of restricting his natural movements, stepped down from the train. Vendors moved up and down the platform hawking newspapers, food, and even "maps of opportunity" that they touted as being the best source for available homesteading claims.

As he made his way toward the eastern end of the platform, the agent saw a small, precise man with curly dark hair wearing a black suit working his way through the crowd. Jared recognized him as Charles Roth, personal secretary to Matthew Faraday. "Mr. Roth? Mr. Roth, are you looking for me?" he called.

Hearing his name, Roth's eyes searched through the crowd until they made contact with Jared. "Ah, Mr. Macalester," the man announced, beaming. "It's good to see you again. Come, I have a carriage waiting for us. Have you any luggage?"

Jared smiled. "No, I always travel light. I've got whatever I need in my valise." Shrugging, he added, "After all, I'm only staying overnight."

Nodding, Roth adjusted the pince-nez on the end of his nose and remarked, "Ah, well, then, we don't have to wait for the luggage to be detrained. Shall we?" He gestured in the direction he had come.

The two men made their way to the front of the depot where an elegant cabriolet sat. Climbing in, the Faraday employees settled in the back seat, discussing away from any prying ears a plan developed by Matthew Faraday.

"Mr. Faraday is transferring a rather large sum of cash to the office in San Francisco," Roth explained.

"So he *is* the one sending the sixty thousand dollars," Jared murmured.

"You know about the money?" Roth asked in surprise.

"I heard it over the wire when I was in the telegraph office," Jared explained. His blue eyes glinting, he looked at Roth sharply. "I take it the money is bait."

"Yes, that's exactly what it is—although no one connected with the railroad knows that. All arrangements were made just as if this were a routine shipment. That way, whoever has been finding out about the money shipments will be able to discover about this shipment in the same manner."

"And attempt to rob the train," Jared concluded.

"Correct."

"Only this time, I'll be aboard, I presume."

"Correct again," Roth confirmed, smiling at Jared as though he were a star pupil. "But not as a guard. A guard would be too visible, and neither Mr. Faraday nor I wish to lose another field operative. You are to travel as a passenger, for that way your presence will be less obvious, and you can keep an eye open."

Nodding, Jared responded, "I understand."

"But please, Mr. Macalester, be careful."

"Oh I intend to be, Mr. Roth. I intend to be."

Her niece fully recovered from her illness, Charlotte Baker was heading back to Ironsprings, and her sister and brother-in-law had accompanied her to the Denver station. Walking alongside the train that would take the publisher home, they made their way to the parlor car that would whisk Charlotte back to Ironsprings in luxury. Her brother-in-law, Martin Davis, had insisted on buying her the first-class return passage; now, in addition, he tried to press five hundred dollars into her hand.

"No," Charlotte told him firmly. "You two have been more than generous to me these last several months. Why, you've already loaned me two thousand dollars."

"No," he corrected, "we didn't loan it to you. We were paying you back."

Charlotte looked at him quizzically. "Paying me back? Don't be silly, Martin. Paying me back for what?"

"Charlotte, do you remember when you traveled with the medicine show how you sent money to us when we needed it?" Martin asked.

Shaking her head, Charlotte reminded him, "Yes, but that was only a few hundred dollars—not two thousand."

"A couple of hundred dollars meant as much for you then as two thousand means for us now," her brother-in-law insisted. "You'd be amazed at how many people are subscribing to our telephone service. Why, I can foresee the day when there will be an instrument in every home."

"Martin is right," Linda stated. "We have more money than we can use, and you need some help in fighting this battle to get your town incorporated. Charlotte, please, if you love me, you'll let us do this for you."

Charlotte looked at the envelope in her hand, then sighed and smiled. Hugging her sister, then her brother-in-law, she acquiesced. "All right. You make it difficult to say no."

The conductor called for final boarding, and the train let out a short blast on the whistle. The redhead hurried toward the parlor car, her sister and brother-in-law flanking her on either side. She had just stepped up onto the vestibule when, with a hiss of air, the brakes were released and the train started rolling slowly.

Walking alongside, keeping pace with the slow-moving train, Linda and Martin Davis waved good-bye.

"Write us and tell us all about your new fella," Linda directed.

Charlotte grimaced. "There's nothing to tell yet."

The train picked up speed, and Charlotte's family fell behind. "Well, when there is something to tell, let us know," Linda called to her.

"I will," she yelled back. "I promise." Waving good-bye one last time, Charlotte stepped inside the car.

From the moment Charlotte was seated in the car, she saw the difference in the way she was treated. The porter deferred to her, and the conductor was extraordinarily polite. But the biggest difference was the car itself. Having ridden the train many times before, she was used to stained and torn upholstery, expectorated tobacco quids on the floor, a worn carpet, and a mélange of indecipherable smells.

This environment offered a total change. The parlor car was not only spotlessly clean and fresh-smelling, it was resplendent in plush upholstery, rich hangings, and handcarved inlaid paneling. Charlotte had never seen anything to match the luxury and elegance of the car, and she thought to herself that its incredible grandeur would be enough to hold her in wonder for the better part of the trip.

"Madam Baker?" a uniformed steward inquired after she had settled into a large, overstuffed chair.

"Yes."

"Welcome aboard, Madam," the steward said, handing her a menu. "The dining car opens for dinner at six o'clock, and you may schedule your meal at anytime between six and eleven."

Opening the menu, she asked, "What time will we reach Cheyenne?"

"At seven oh-five," he replied, speaking as if the time of arrival was an absolute.

"I'll wait to dine until after we leave Cheyenne," she informed him equally crisply.

"Very well. Shall we say about eight?"

"That will be fine."

"And would Madam Baker care to select from the menu?"

She scanned its pages. Vastly unlike the sack lunches or the very unappetizing fare served at stations along the way, the descriptions of the feasts offered in the gold-embossed menu almost made Charlotte salivate. The menu featured blue-winged teal, antelope steaks, roasted beef, boiled ham and tongue, broiled chicken, fresh vegetables and fruit, and freshly baked rolls and cornbread.

"I'll have broiled chicken, please," she finally announced, returning the menu to the steward.

"An excellent choice," he assured her. "Your dinner will be ready at eight. Enjoy your trip."

After the steward left, Charlotte settled back in her chair and watched the beautiful scenery through the large window. As the train sped northward, huge purple mountains mushroomed in the distance, while in the meadows and plains alongside the track, wildflowers grew in colorful profusion. At first she could not take her eyes from the view, but finally she settled back to read the free newspaper offered by the train, observing it from a strictly professional perspective.

As soon as Jared Macalester and Charles Roth had finished discussing their plans, Matthew Faraday's assistant returned to Kansas City. Since Jared had to wait until the following day for the westbound train that would return him to Ironsprings, he decided to make good use of his time in the territorial capital of Wyoming.

Midmorning the following day, as the train bearing Charlotte was somewhere between Denver and Cheyenne, Jared Macalester climbed the steps of the capitol building and made his way to the governor's office. Approaching the desk of the governor's secretary, he introduced himself and requested an appointment.

With the air of someone who by virtue of his proximity to a person of prominence and importance has assumed some of those qualities himself, the man shook his head and smiled with amusement. "As I'm sure I don't need to point out to you, Mr. Macalester, the governor is a very busy man. You may wait if you wish, but I really don't think the governor will be able to see you today." He gestured at the six other people waiting in the anteroom. "As you can see, there are several others waiting to see him ahead of you."

"I'm also a very busy man," Jared countered, his tone acerbic. "Perhaps if you could just slip me in, we two busy men could get our business over with quickly."

The appointments secretary laughed hollowly. "You are very funny, Mr. Macalester. But, I assure you, if you see the governor at all, it will be when I say you may see him."

Handing the secretary a small white business card, the agent requested firmly, "Would you give him this, please?"

"Yes, I will." The secretary put it down on his desk.

"Now, please," Jared insisted. "Give it to him now."

"Really, Mr. Macalester, I can't be bothered with—"

Cutting in, Jared told him forcefully, "I think the governor would like to see this card now."

The secretary picked the card up and looked at it. "I don't understand. This isn't your card." He started to put it back down again, but Jared's bearing indicated he was not to be trifled with, and, with a long-suffering sigh, he stood. "Very well, Mr. Macalester, I will give the governor this card. Wait here."

Less than a minute later, the governor himself came

out of his office, trailed by the appointments secretary, whose self-importance had clearly been deflated.

"Governor, I'm sorry," the secretary was saying. "I had no idea . . ."

"Mr. Macalester?" the governor asked, extending his hand warmly. "How is my dear friend Matthew?"

"He's fine, Governor, just fine," Jared responded. "Oh, may I have the card back?"

"Yes, yes, of course," the governor said. Holding the card out beyond his ample girth, he stroked his dark walrus mustache and chuckled, reading aloud, "'I would count it as a personal favor if you would see the bearer of this card.'" He chuckled again. "Mr. Macalester, I believe that card would get you in to see the president of the United States. There aren't too many people in a position of authority today who don't owe a favor to Matthew Faraday."

Smiling, Jared retrieved the card and admitted, "As a matter of fact, Governor, I believe some of my fellow agents have used this device to see the president on occasion."

The governor ushered the agent into his office. "In that case, I can do no less. Come, Mr. Macalester, tell me what I can do for you."

The door shut behind him, and as the two men crossed the floor to the enormous desk that dominated the room, Jared scanned the richly paneled walls decorated with plaques and photographs. Sitting down across the desk from the governor, Jared told him about his investigation of the series of train robberies.

When the agent had finished, the governor shook his head angrily and stared at Jared across his enormous desk. "These robberies are not only troublesome for the railroad, they are a blight on the territory of Wyoming. Mr. Macalester, if there's anything I can do that will help you in your investigation—anything at all—you have only to ask."

"I'm glad you said that. As a matter of fact, sir, I would like a temporary appointment as a territorial marshal. I don't need the pay, but I do want the authority."

"You shall have it," the governor declared without question.

"And I want you to grant immediate incorporation status for Ironsprings—that is, as soon as they can arrange a vote."

"Very well. Have a seat in the waiting room, and I'll instruct the secretary of state to issue a certificate of charter bearing my signature to take with you," the governor offered. "The moment the vote is taken, have the results telegraphed to the secretary of state here in Cheyenne. Assuming that the citizenry will vote for a legalized status, the receipt of that telegram will automatically activate Ironsprings as an incorporated town."

"Thank you, Governor," Jared said, standing and extending his hand. "You've been most helpful."

"No, the territory of Wyoming owes its thanks to you and to the Faraday Security Agency for taking on a problem we should have undertaken ourselves long ago," the governor replied. "By the way, I would consider it a pleasure if you would have dinner with me this evening—say around eight?"

"Thank you, Governor, I would enjoy that," Jared replied. "But I'll be on the train for Ironsprings by then."

Ushering his visitor toward the door, the governor murmured, "Yes, yes, of course. Well, Mr. Macalester, I wish you all the luck in the world with this case. And please do give my regards to Matthew Faraday next time you communicate with him."

"I will indeed, sir."

Deputy Billy Wade sat at his desk in the marshal's office in Ironsprings, staring at one of the posters his brother had been studying the night he was killed. Although Billy had not noticed it before, Adam had written some notes on the back of the flyer, and he was trying to decipher their meaning.

"'Dressed different in SW,'" he mumbled. "'Was wearing gun. Playing cards with railroad telegrapher. Could have been getting information. Would not ride back to Ironsprings with me.'"

Looking up, Billy asked Josh, who was sitting across from him, "Did Adam say anything to you about anyone he met over in Sweetwater?"

The marshal put down the revolver he had been cleaning and shook his head. "No. Why?"

"He's got some notes scribbled on the back of one of these posters, and I have a feeling they have something to do with what he was working on."

"Workin' on?" Josh laughed scornfully. "Billy, don't get me wrong. Adam was my brother, too, and I loved him as much as you did. But he wasn't real bright."

Glaring at his brother, Billy replied, "Josh, sometimes you can be real troublesome. You think you're so smart that you never give anyone else credit for having a lick of sense."

The marshal's eyebrows shot up. "So you think Adam had an idea who was behind these robberies?"

"I'm not saying he was right," Billy confessed, "but at least he had an idea. That's more than we have."

Josh looked at his younger brother intently. "Who did he think it was?"

Sighing, Billy admitted, "I don't know. But if I can find out who he saw over in Sweetwater, I'd have a good notion."

The marshal put his gun down and leaned back in his chair. "All right. How do you propose to find out?"

Billy ran an impatient hand through his thick sandy hair. "Maybe by doing my job, Josh. Maybe by doing a little police work."

Josh laughed scornfully.

"I can see that you're really interested," Billy retorted angrily.

"I'm sorry," the marshal responded, controlling his laughter. "Look, you go ahead and do your police work. If you can find out something, I'm all for it.

Maybe that would change people's minds about this incorporation business."

"Fine," Billy agreed, standing and grabbing his Stetson. He strode toward the door and called over his shoulder, "I'll see you later."

Pulling the door shut behind him, Billy turned to his left and headed toward the depot. He then went inside and walked over to the telegraph counter, finding Carl Masters reading a newspaper.

The telegrapher looked up when he heard the deputy enter and declared, "I tell you, Billy, you can sure tell the difference in the paper 'round here when Charlotte Baker's gone. Since she left Johnny Rogers in charge, seems like he ain't done nothin' more'n reprint things they did a long time ago. Why, there's news in here that's three months old." He folded the paper and set it aside. "What can I do for you?"

"Carl, do you know the railroad telegrapher in Sweetwater?"

"Sure. His name's Titus Moore. I've known Titus a long time."

"I want you to ask him who he was playing cards with on the second of this month. I'm especially interested in knowing if someone from Ironsprings might have been in that game."

The old man looked at the deputy curiously. "What? That seems like a strange request. What if he don't remember . . . or don't want to say?"

Billy leaned across the counter and said emphatically, "It's real important, Carl. The man he was playing cards with might be one of the men who's been robbing the trains."

"What makes you think a thing like that?"

"I've got my reasons," Billy replied. "Just ask him, will you?"

Shrugging, Carl told him, "Sure. But that'll cost the same as sendin' any other message."

"I'll pay."

"All right. You want to spend your money like that, I guess you got a right," Carl intoned. He moved over to the telegraph instrument, released the key, then cleared the line for a message. When the clearance came back to him, he started sending. There was silence for a few moments, then the key started clacking again.

Turning in his chair, Carl read the answer he had just received. "Titus says he played cards with two fellas from over here on that day. One was your brother, Adam. The other was Johnny Rogers."

"Damn! Johnny Rogers! Of course! That would be why Adam thought it significant enough to write something like that down," Billy exclaimed.

"What are you talkin' about, Billy? Are you saying Johnny Rogers has been robbin' the trains?"

Looking at the telegrapher sternly, Billy warned, "Don't you say anything to anybody about this." He paused, then asked, "By the way, how much for the message?"

"Seventy-five cents."

Billy pulled the silver from his pocket and laid it on the counter, then left the depot and started toward the newspaper office. His mind was whirling the whole way, thinking about everything connected with the robberies—and especially the things that Jared Macalester had told him. Reaching his destination, he pushed open the front door, and Johnny looked up from the press.

"Hello, Billy," the youth said warmly, smiling broadly at the deputy. "What can I do for you?"

"You can put your hands up," Billy responded, pulling his pistol.

"Billy, what the hell is this?" Josh Wade demanded, completely bewildered, when his brother escorted the prisoner into the marshal's office. "What's goin' on?"

Pushing the youth toward the cell area, Billy explained, "I'm arresting Johnny Rogers for train robbery. He's the one Adam saw over in Sweetwater."

"So?"

"Well, think about it, Josh," Billy told his brother

impatiently. "Sweetwater is where the train was supposed to get water . . . but it didn't. I think Johnny was over there making the arrangements. Adam didn't know about the water tank, of course, but he figured out something was going on—and he figured out that Johnny was right in the middle of it. But before he could put it all together, Johnny waited for him in an alley and shot him."

Throwing up his hands in protest, Johnny bleated, "No, Billy, I didn't do no such thing! You're crazy!"

"You'll have a chance to tell it to a judge," Billy promised, trying to control his rage.

"He won't need to," Josh corrected. "We're gonna let him go."

Disbelieving his ears, the deputy shouted, "What? Now, hold on, Josh, don't be a fool. You know the vest I was talking to you about? The one I loaned to Charlotte? It all adds up now. Johnny could've easily gotten it. He's over there all the time."

"I said, let him go," Josh ordered.

Billy glared at Josh, a mixture of shock and anger coursing through him. Then, sighing with frustration, he put his pistol back in his holster and sat down.

Johnny smiled at Billy. "Don't worry about it, Deputy. I ain't holding no hard feelings for you. Now, if you fellas will excuse me, I gotta get the paper out. Mrs. Baker will be back in town tomorrow morning, and I don't want her to think I wasn't doing my job."

As soon as the door shut behind Johnny, Billy leaned across the desk and demanded, "Why didn't you at least let me explain."

"Explain what?" Josh scoffed. "Johnny Rogers couldn't have done it."

"Adam must've thought so," Billy countered. "And thinking that got him killed."

"Billy," Josh explained calmly, "if you'd bothered to come check with me before you flew off the handle, I could've told you that Johnny Rogers was in the Pleasure Palace when Adam was shot. There was a party that night, remember? There are probably a dozen witnesses who can put him there."

The deputy shook his head. "Damn!"

"I told you to leave the train robberies alone," Josh reminded him. "Hell, they're Macalester's worry, not ours."

Chapter 11

THE WESTBOUND TRAIN HAD FINALLY PULLED OUT OF THE Cheyenne station shortly before eight o'clock, and as Jared Macalester stood just inside the vestibule of the dining car, waiting to be shown to a table, he idly gazed through the door that separated the car from the parlor car behind it. To his surprise and delight, Charlotte Baker was making her way through the parlor car, heading his way. Deciding to surprise her as well, he positioned himself slightly off to one side. When the redhead entered the car, she was immediately met by the steward, but before he could show her to her table, Jared Macalester walked up to her and smiled.

"Jared!" she exclaimed, looking pleased. "What are you doing here?"

Skirting the truth, the agent replied, "I'm about to have dinner with you. That is, if you would join me at my table."

"Of course," Charlotte agreed.

The steward beamed at them, escorting them

through the car. Stopping in the middle of the car, he gestured at an elegantly set table. "Madam, sir..."

Jared held out her chair. She sat down, smoothing the folds of her deep-green serge traveling outfit, then declared as he sat down opposite her, "Well, I must confess, I never expected to see you here. What a wonderful surprise this is."

The Faraday man merely smiled, then picked up his folded linen napkin and flicked it open, placing it on his lap. "How are things with your sister's family?" he asked.

Charlotte was clearly pleased by his obvious concern. "Fine," she replied. "My niece is well again, and things are back to normal."

"I'm glad," he told her softly. "Oh, I have something for you." He reached into his inside jacket pocket and took out an envelope.

"What is it?" Charlotte asked.

Extracting the incorporation charter from the envelope, Jared laid it on the table in front of her. "It already has the governor's signature," he pointed out.

Reading it quickly, Charlotte's face reflected the pleasure she felt. "Jared," she breathed, "this is..." She stopped.

"I know," he groaned, grimacing. "Not worth the paper it's printed on, until a majority of the people vote for it." Waggling his forefinger, he added, "But the moment the vote is counted and validated, a telegram to Cheyenne will activate it."

The publisher shook her head, telling him flatly, "Well, you're completely wrong when you say it isn't worth the paper it's printed on. And I was going to say no such thing. Why, with this, I can get the vote out. Don't you see? This will prove that it can be done. How on earth did you ever get this?"

"I asked for it," Jared said simply.

"You asked for it—and that's all it took?"

"If you know how to ask," Jared chuckled.

Looking at the agent questioningly, the redhead

queried, "And how on earth did you know I was going to be on this train? Did you ask someone about that, too?"

Leaning back, Jared looked at her, amused. "Let's call it luck."

Their eyes locked, and Charlotte blushed slightly. "I'm really pleased you came to meet me," she told him in a slightly breathy voice. "It will make the trip back to Ironsprings very pleasant."

Their meals were served, and for the next hour most of their conversation revolved around food. Sipping coffee at the end of their sumptuous repasts, Charlotte explained how she came to be in a parlor car for the trip back, inviting Jared to join her.

"Would you believe it?" she asked. "There are only two other people in that entire car. And just before I left to come to dinner, I heard them ask the porter to make their beds, so we'd be quite alone. You will join me, won't you?"

Jared felt his heartbeat quicken. "Who could resist an offer like that?" he replied.

Finishing their coffee, they left the dining car and made their way back to the parlor car. When they entered, they found that while it was not totally dark, the car was very dim, its only light coming from a lamp at each end of the car, both of which were turned way down. Walking through the car, they passed by the curtained berths of the couple Charlotte had referred to, and she smiled and put her finger across her lips as she pointed to where they were sleeping.

Quietly, they tiptoed past the heavy green drapery, then went down to the far end of the car where an overstuffed sofa and a group of large chairs made up the sitting area.

"You know," Charlotte whispered as they sat on the sofa, "there's another reason I'm glad you're here. I'm carrying a rather large sum of money, and it makes me feel safer to know that I have someone with me."

"I wouldn't think you would need me, seeing as you're the greatest female pistoleer in the West," he blurted.

Charlotte suddenly laughed, then covered her mouth in embarrassment as she glanced toward the berths at the other end of the car. Keeping her voice down, she demanded, "Where did you hear that? Did Billy tell you?" She shook her head in mock anger. "I swore him to secrecy, too. Well, so much for trusting a man to keep quiet. It was all phony, you know. I couldn't hit the side of the barn."

The agent's eyes narrowed, and he remarked, "But you *were* a trick-shot artist for a medicine show."

"Yes, and my marksmanship was about as valid as the medicine," Charlotte quipped. "I broke glass bottles using pistols loaded with birdshot. All I had to do was point in the same general direction. Anyone could have done it . . . with their eyes closed." She laughed again. "I have to admit, though, it was a lot of fun. Until Cap exposed me."

"Cap exposed you?" Jared was clearly surprised.

Charlotte's eyes were filled with amusement. "He did a story about the one dollar a bottle elixir and the phony trick-shot artist. The medicine show left town, but I stayed behind . . . and married Cap Baker." Her face looked wistful for a brief moment, but then the look passed.

Jared decided to get the answer to another question that troubled him. "You said you were carrying a lot of money. Why?"

Waving a dismissive hand in front of her face, the redhead explained, "It's embarrassing, really. You see, my brother-in-law has always been one to invest in get-rich-quick schemes, but none of them ever worked out. In fact, there were occasions when Martin's impetuousness caused some pretty lean times for Linda and their kids. Well, I couldn't let my sister and her children starve, so I helped out when I was able, sending what money I could spare—even before I married Cap. And then, after Cap and I were married, he pitched in, too."

A wry smile wreathed her mouth as she continued, "They say God protects fools and drunks, and there must be something to it, because my brother-in-law's most recent investment seems to be paying off. He owns the Denver telephone system, and he already has over five hundred subscribers. Over the last couple of months he and Linda have felt obligated to share their good fortune with me. They gave me the money to pay off the building I'm in now and to buy some new type for my printing press. I told them I don't need anything else, but just before I left Denver they gave me another five hundred dollars to make up for the lost revenue from the merchants who have quit advertising with me."

The relief that Jared felt seemed to visibly buoy him up, and he found himself sitting a bit straighter on the sofa. Thinking of the large bank deposits Charlotte had made, he smiled to himself and murmured, "So, that explains it."

"That explains what?" she wanted to know.

"Why I had the good fortune to meet you," he lied easily. "You just said God protects fools and idiots." Reaching for her, Jared pulled Charlotte to him and kissed her, hesitantly at first and then with fervor.

"Damn!" Grub swore.

"What is it?" Tucker asked.

"I just barked my shin. That moon's good and bright up top, but down here, I can't see a damn thing."

"Will you two quit the gabbin' and get them charges planted?" Tim Quick growled. Looking eastward, he stood on the railroad track at the North Platte River, keeping his eyes peeled for the westbound train. The three robbers had ridden to the crossing, and Grub and Tucker had crawled out onto the trestle bridging the river. Quick's two underlings were now on the underpinnings, placing a couple of bundles of dynamite.

"It ain't all that easy to do it in the dark," Grub complained loudly.

"Well, did you want to do it in the daylight when anyone in the world who wanted to could've seen you?"

"I guess not," Grub agreed. He then directed his cohort, "Tucker, hand me that there fuse."

The men worked diligently for a few more minutes, then Grub declared, "Finished!" They climbed carefully up from the beams and braces and made their way back onto the tracks, aware of the river some twenty feet below.

When the men reached the spot where Quick was waiting, the gunslinger grumbled, "Took you long enough."

Ignoring him, Tucker asked, "Tim, we plannin' on settin' off this charge while the train is actually on the trestle?"

"No, after it's already crossed over," Quick answered, sarcastically. "Of course we're going to set it off while the train is on the trestle. That's the only way we can be sure to stop it."

"What if you done it before the train got there? The engineer'd still have to stop."

Snorting, Quick gestured behind them with his thumb, replying, "And maybe throw the thing in reverse and back all the way to Cheyenne, leavin' us standin' here like a bunch of jackasses? We'll set it off when the train is right over it, just like I planned."

"All right, if you say so," Tucker said without much enthusiasm.

"You don't like that?"

The man shrugged. "I was just thinkin' of all the people that's liable to get killed, that's all. You know me, Tim. In a shoot-out, it don't bother me none to kill someone. Hell, I could kill anyone in a shoot-out. But these here people is just dirt farmers and store clerks. And there's bound to be women and kids, too."

Planting his hands on his hips, Quick snarled, "So what?"

"I was just thinkin', is all."

"Yeah? Well don't think." Staring unwaveringly at Tucker, he advised, "If you want to pull out of this, go ahead. Me and Grub'll be glad to split your share of the money."

The man sighed. "Okay, I'm with you. Don't worry, I'll do my part."

"Good." Quick flashed an evil smile. "And just to show you that I believe you, I'm going to let you set off the explosion."

"Oh, Tim, no, I don't know . . ." Tucker's face blanched.

"You don't have no choice in the matter," Quick admonished, his voice harsh. "It's gonna be you that sets off the blast, and you that kills all the people that's gonna get killed." His hand dropped toward his holster. "Unless you want to argue about it with me."

"No, no, I'll do it," Tucker quickly agreed.

"I figured you would," Quick laughed humorlessly. He lifted his hand and pulled his hat down tighter. "Anyway, don't worry about it. After the dynamite goes off, things'll be easy. We'll just climb down to where the wrecked train is, take the money out of the safe in the mail car, and be on our way."

"What if they have armed guards?" Grub asked.

"What if they do?" Quick asked. He giggled. "They can't do a hell of a lot of good if they're down there under the wreckage with everyone else. I tell you, all we have to do is just pick up the money and ride the hell out of here."

Suddenly Tucker hissed urgently, "The train!"

They all stood stock still and listened, hearing a sound in the distance as yet so far away that it was almost as if it were the lonely sigh of wind over an open prairie rather than the whistle of a distant train.

"Okay, you two," Quick ordered as he ran for cover, "get ready."

* * *

The kissing had nearly gotten out of hand, their first long and passionate kiss followed by another and then another. Only the fact that Charlotte Baker and Jared Macalester were in a semipublic place held them in check.

Finally, with a loud sigh, Charlotte pushed herself away and started straightening her clothes.

"Look at me! What you must think of me," she moaned. "I'm behaving like a buffalo gal on a Saturday night."

Jared grinned, and the smile was decidedly amorous. Cupping her chin in his hand, he whispered hoarsely, "What I think of you is that you are the most desirable woman I have ever known. And I have missed you far more than I ever thought I would."

"I missed you, too," she whispered back.

They kissed again; then Charlotte rested her head on his shoulder and let him hold her that way for a long while. Finally she lifted her head up and looked at him. "Jared," she asked, breaking the silence, "when you're finished with this case, where will you go?"

Shrugging, he replied, "I don't know. I suppose it depends on where Matthew Faraday sends me."

"Oh, I don't mean where will Faraday send you. I mean, where will you live?"

He thought for a moment, then told her, "I guess I'll go back to Cheyenne."

"You wouldn't have to, you know," she remarked in a somewhat tentative voice. "You could live in Ironsprings. After all, you're always gone one place or another anyway, so the place you come home to could be anywhere you want it to be."

Suddenly feeling on the defensive, he allowed, without too much conviction, "I suppose it could."

Charlotte laughed. "Listen, I don't want you to think I'm trying to get you pinned down to something like marriage," she assured him. "The truth is, I'm not sure I'm ready for it. This newspaper means a lot to me—maybe more than anything else in the world.

Maybe even more than you could." She gazed into his eyes, her face growing serious. "But I do know this. I don't want you to go away."

Relaxing a bit, Jared remarked, "Maybe I won't go away. That is, if you understand from the beginning that I'm not ready for anything like marriage."

"Understand? I'd insist upon it," Charlotte said, touching his cheek gently. "Just as I insist upon another kiss," she added.

When the conductor came into the car a few moments later to check the lamps, his sudden and unexpected appearance surprised Jared and Charlotte, and they separated quickly. They were quite sure the man did not see them locked in their passionate embrace—or, if he did, he tactfully pretended not to.

"Conductor, where are we?" Jared asked. He looked out through the window, but he could see nothing except darkness and the squares of yellow light reflected from the windows traveling along with them.

"We're about ten miles from the North Platte River, sir," the conductor answered, then hurried through the car.

"The North Platte!" the Faraday man exclaimed, snapping his fingers and getting to his feet. "That's where they'll hit us. I know it is!"

"What are you talking about? That's where who will hit us?" the redhead asked in bewilderment.

"The train robbers. This train is carrying a great deal of money," Jared explained, "and I believe it's going to be robbed. When it is, I intend to catch the robbers."

An expression of realization came across Charlotte's face. "You weren't on this train to meet me, were you?"

"That would have been my choice of reasons," Jared bantered. Then he admitted soberly, "But, no." He took her right hand and kissed it. "I have to hurry up to the engine."

Charlotte smiled, assuring him, "I'll still be here when it's all finished."

The agent pivoted and raced out of the parlor car. Walking one by one through the various passenger cars, he then reached the mail car. After giving a prearranged series of knocks, Jared waited a moment. When the door opened, he was met by the clerk and a guard carrying a double-barreled shotgun.

"Is everything all right?" the agent asked of the guard, an employee of the Union Pacific to whom Jared had introduced himself in Cheyenne.

"Everything's fine, Mr. Macalester," the man, a twenty-year veteran of the railroad, assured him. "Anyone who tries to come through any of these doors without the right signal is going to get a face full of buckshot," the guard promised.

"Are you going to stay here with us?" the clerk asked.

Gesturing toward the front of the train, Jared told him, "No, I'm going on up to the engine. If anything does happen, I figure that's the earliest place to learn about it."

"Be careful climbing across the tender," the clerk warned.

Jared looked back over his shoulder and smiled crookedly. "Don't worry, I will."

He made his way out the far door and stood on the platform behind the wood tender. He stared at the obstacle for a long moment, not relishing having to scurry across it at night while traveling better than thirty miles per hour.

Out here the noise was deafening, and the wind very strong. Looking down, he could see the crossties flashing beneath him. Taking a deep breath, he resolutely grabbed hold of the ladder, climbed to the top, scrambled nimbly across the pile of wood, then finally dropped down onto the platform behind the engineer and fireman.

The engineer turned and acknowledged him. Forewarned by the agent about his suspicions, the crewman said gruffly, "Well, Macalester, does your sudden company mean what I think it does?"

"Yeah. I'm convinced that they're going to try and hit us at the North Platte."

Shaking his head, the engineer faced forward again. "Then I guess we'd better get ready, 'cause we'll be crossing the North Platte in about two minutes."

True to the engineer's word, the train soon approached a long trestle, then clacked out onto it. It had gone only a few yards when suddenly the bridge exploded just up ahead, erupting into a sheet of flame.

"Jump!" the engineer screamed, and without waiting for a second invitation, Jared leapt out into the black maw alongside the track. He fell for what seemed an interminable time. Finally there was the shock of cold water, and sinking far below the surface, he realized that he had leapt all the way over the edge of the trestle, into the river.

Feeling that his lungs were about to burst, he fought his way back up to the surface, popping out of the water just as the boiler of the engine exploded in a brilliant burst of white followed by a cloud of billowing steam. The locomotive fell through the gap in the bridge, and the cars all followed, twisting, wrenching, and tearing off the tracks. One by one they rushed over the jagged edge of the destroyed trestle, crashing with a thunderous roar to the riverbank below and piling up in a heap, pushing the engine and the tender into the river. For fully thirty seconds, cars piled upon cars to the sounds of timber snapping, metal squealing, and glass shattering. Finally there was a deathly silence for a few seconds; then came the snap and crack of flames as the cars caught fire.

Seeing that the parlor car had been crushed between two other cars, Jared screamed, "Charlotte!" He swam for the riverbank, then scrambled out of the water and started picking his way across the rocks and through the fallen timbers of the destroyed trestle toward the wrecked train.

As he neared the first car, Jared heard soft moaning,

and the cries were so low and indistinct that he did not know if they were coming from a man or a woman. He was about to attempt entry into the car when the air was split with a triumphant cry.

"Yahoo! Did you see that?" a familiar voice shouted. "Come on, let's get the money and skedaddle out of here!"

Jared froze where he was, then turned toward the sound of the voice. He saw two men working their way down to the wreck while a third sat his horse on top of the embankment.

"Where's the mail car, Tim?" one of the men yelled. "Can you see it?"

"Yeah, it's the first car near the river," Quick answered.

Even if he had not heard the name, Jared would have easily recognized the voice.

"Quick, you son of a bitch!" the agent shouted, his anger getting the better of him. "You did this!"

"It's Macalester!" one of the two men approaching the wrecked cars yelled. "I see him! Over there!"

Tucker and Grub dropped to their knees and fired, and Jared jumped to the ground. Flashes of orange lit the darkness, the bullets sparking like fireworks as they hit the rocks. They shot repeatedly, and flying lead whistled through the air and whined off stone, but all their shots went wild.

One of the outlaws suddenly stood up and looked around, trying to determine their prey's whereabouts, and his shadow loomed large against the embankment. He offered Jared an easy shot, and the agent watched the man go down after he fired.

"What the hell!" an anguished voice exclaimed. "Quick! Quick, he got Grub!"

Jared heard the scratch of hooves on gravel, and when he looked up at the top of the embankment, he saw a rider heading away.

"Quick, you cowardly son of a bitch!" the gunslinger's cohort yelled, standing up and firing wildly at the man riding off.

"Tucker!" Jared called to him. "Tucker, give it up. There's just you and me now! Throw down your gun!"

"The hell I will!" Tucker screamed, and he swung back around toward the Faraday man and fired again. His slug hit the ground to Jared's left, and the agent returned fire. Tucker crumpled with a bullet in his chest.

Scrambling over to him to make certain he posed no further threat, Jared looked down at Tucker, his shirt covered with blood, which looked black in the moonlight.

"Help me," Tucker pleaded.

"Give me some answers first," Jared growled. He looked around, then demanded, "Where's your other buddy—the one you call Logan?"

Gasping for air, Tucker replied, "Dead. Quick shot him."

Jared looked at the man with a start. Then his eyes narrowed, and he demanded, "Who else has Quick killed? Was he the one who shot Adam Wade?"

"No. Leastwise, he said he didn't. But he did write the note."

Shaking his head, the agent asked, "Why? What did he hope to gain?"

Tucker laughed. "Quick don't need much reason to do nothin'," he allowed. "He said he did it so's to cause trouble between the Wades and the Stockards. He thought it was a real good joke, accusin' George Stockard of the killin'." Suddenly the outlaw's hand reached toward Jared Macalester as if he were asking for supplication. Then it fell onto his lap, and Tucker lay still.

As safely as he could, Jared picked his way through the wreck, horrified at the carnage. Burning lamps had begun to ignite parts of the splintered, twisted cars into a colossal bonfire. Even those people who had been relatively uninjured in the crash were in a critical situation, because many were trapped in the wreckage with no way to escape the encroaching flames.

The engineer and fireman managed to work their

way back to the riverbank and stood on top of the embankment, momentarily frozen with shock and staring helplessly at the wreckage. Then one of them yelled to Jared, "Are you all right?"

"Yes!" Jared answered. "Come on, we've got to get these people out of here!"

The Faraday man tried to open the door of one of the cars, but it was jammed from the fall and could not be budged. The car was already on fire, and through the windows he could see the dazed passengers, their state of shock not allowing them fully to comprehend their danger.

"Hey!" someone yelled from above. "There's a switchman's shack up here with some tools in it. Could you use an ax?"

Jared lifted his head. "Throw it down!"

"Here it comes!"

The ax came clattering down the embankment, striking sparks off the rocks. Grabbing it, the agent then began chopping at the side of the wooden car. The fireman and engineer finally reached his side, and as soon as he had a hole big enough for those trapped inside to squirm through, Jared reached inside and began helping them out, with the uninjured crewmen lending their assistance.

When it finally appeared that the last of the passengers had been extricated from the wrecked car, Jared stuck his head inside and yelled into the smoky interior, "Is anyone else in here?"

There was a brief pause, and then a woman's voice responded from deep inside the car, her words indistinct. The agent kept calling to her, directing her with his voice toward the opening. Her cries became louder as she neared him, and finally Jared saw her, and he thrust his arms through the hole, shouting, "Here! Give me your hands!"

"My daughter! My daughter!" the woman screamed hysterically, grabbing at the agent's sleeve. "She's trapped in there. Please! You must get her out!"

He pulled her through the opening, making sure she was safe, then started into the car.

"Macalester!" the engineer shouted. "In about one more minute this thing's going to be burning like a torch. If you go in, you won't make it out."

"Then *I'm* going back for her!" the woman shrieked, and she started back inside. But Jared pulled her away.

"You wait here," he ordered. "I'll get your daughter out of there. Where were you sitting?"

"I was about halfway back, on the lefthand side." She began whimpering. "The side that's on the bottom now."

"The fire's already reached there," the engineer cautioned, shaking his head in dismay.

The Faraday man again started into the hole. "I've got to try," he insisted. He squirmed in through the hole, then stood for a moment to get his bearings. Eerily lit by the encroaching flames, the car was so filled with smoke that it was hard to breathe.

Picking his way through the car, the agent tripped over something, and he looked down. It was a leg. Shifting his gaze to the man's face, the open, staring eyes told Jared immediately that the passenger was beyond help.

"Hello!" he called, regretting that he had neglected to ask the child's name or her age. He had no idea whether the child was old enough to respond to his voice, even if she was conscious and could hear.

"Hello!" he called again. "Anyone in here?"

"I can't get loose," a small, frightened voice replied.

"Where are you, darling?"

"I'm here," the voice answered.

Squinting through the swirling smoke, Jared tried to pinpoint the child's location. "Ah, there you are," he finally breathed when he saw the little girl. She was pinned beneath an overturned seat but miraculously, the very thing that held her trapped had also saved her life. A heavy steel axle from one of the other cars had crashed through the roof, but the stiff wooden seat had prevented it from crushing the child.

Making his way to her as quickly as he could, he felt the heat of the flames that were already scorching the seat behind the child, although she was somewhat protected by the shield of the overturned seat. Jared put his shoulder against the axle and strained with all his might, trying to move it, but it would not budge. Then he tried to pry up the seat, but he failed again. Desperate, he looked around frantically, finally noticing a length of rail that had broken off and was sticking through the side of the car. Picking up the rail, he wedged it under the seat and pried so hard that the veins stood out on his neck. He was rewarded by a slight movement.

Resting for a moment, he looked down at the little girl and panted, "Are you hurt anywhere?"

"No," the child replied, but she began whimpering.

Jared realized then that the shock, which had been keeping the little girl reasonably calm, was beginning to wear off. If she panicked now, he never would get her out of here.

"Honey, you're going to have to help me," he explained softly. "When I move the seat, you slide out from under it. All right?"

"All right."

Positioning his hands just so, Jared then put all his strength into the lever, and the seat rose a few inches. "Now!" he called.

The child scrambled out from under the seat, and the moment she was clear, Jared let it fall. He reached down and picked her up in his arms, commanding, "Hold tight!" With her arms wrapped around his neck, he rushed back through the thickening smoke to the hole in the side of the car. At his shout, hands reached in and he gave the little girl up to them. Then he wriggled out behind her.

The passengers who had gathered around the train to await the outcome of the drama let out a lusty cheer. Gasping desperately for air, the Faraday man hardly noticed.

"Jared! Jared, are you all right?" a woman's voice asked.

Whipping his head around, Jared breathed a sigh of relief as Charlotte Baker came toward him, smiling and, happily, unhurt. They fell into each others' arms and clung tightly to each other for a long moment. Then, as if reading the other's thoughts, they separated and began helping those less fortunate than themselves.

Jared climbed up the embankment to the trestle, and he was pleased to discover that although there was a gaping hole on the right side of the bridge, the left side was intact enough to walk across. The Faraday man scurried back down the embankment and began mustering the able-bodied passengers, instructing some to tend the injured and others to assist him. Using tabletops and drapes, makeshift stretchers were made, and the injured were hauled up to the tracks and carried across the bridge to the other side of the North Platte River.

When the most critical rescue effort was completed, Jared climbed a telegraph pole and sent word ahead to the next station of the train wreck. Within a short while, a rescue train arrived from the west, carrying doctors, blankets, and first-aid supplies. Soon afterward, the rescue train beat its way back down the track, bearing both injured and uninjured passengers. In Rawlins, the injured went to the hospital, while those able enough to travel connected with a new train and continued their journey.

Weary and filthy, Jared Macalester and Charlotte Baker sat wordlessly beside each other as the rescue train bore them toward their destination. Jared had been surprised to find the mail car had sustained little damage, and he was able to retrieve the satchel filled with money. Now, the bag of money sitting safely at his feet, the agent sat with his arm around the publisher's shoulder, and it was just before dawn when the train finally reached Ironsprings. The couple were the only passengers getting off there, and they climbed down from the train onto a deserted platform.

They watched the train as it pulled out of the station, continuing its western run, until the green and red lamps on the last car were but tiny dots in the distance. When the train at last receded, they were left in utter quiet.

"Come on," Charlotte sighed, "I'll fix us some breakfast."

Arm in arm, Jared and Charlotte walked down the street from the depot to her house. Jared glanced at her from time to time, thinking how glad he was that she had not been hurt in the accident—and how not for many years had any woman affected him as this one did.

Chapter 12

JARED MACALESTER AND CHARLOTTE BAKER ARRIVED AT her house, their long journey finally over, and as they walked up the pathway to her door, the publisher stuck her hand into her reticule to take out the latchkey. Suddenly, from out of the shadows, Tim Quick leapt in front of them. Wrapping one arm around Charlotte's neck, he cupped his hand over her mouth. In his other hand he held a pistol, and he pointed it at the redhead's temple.

"Well, now," he chortled, eyeing the satchel, "I see you brought the money to me. That was damn good of you, Macalester."

Angry at himself for not remaining alert, thereby endangering Charlotte—who was his primary concern—Jared growled, "I should've known you'd show up, Quick."

Quick sneered, "Just like I knew you'd be bringin' the money back with you ... assumin' it hadn't burned up." Laughing evilly, he added, "That sure was one hell of a wreck—and it sure felt good to get the better of a Faraday man."

Jared stared at the gunslinger. "So you know who I am, eh?"

Sniffing derisively, Quick said, "Oh, yeah, I know, all right. That's why I didn't have to stick around and see if the money was rescued—and who done the rescuin'." He grinned. "It sure made things a whole lot simpler. I just had to hightail it back here and wait to see if you showed up carryin' that there bag. And damn if you ain't done just that."

He abruptly shoved Charlotte away, then held out his hand, curling his fingers in a beckoning motion. "Give me the money," he demanded, pointing the pistol in his other hand at Jared.

"All right," Jared agreed, his voice resigned, and he tossed the satchel gently toward Quick, hoping to keep the gunman from getting agitated.

Then—so fast and unexpected that Quick was not even aware, until it was too late, that he was in danger—Jared drew his pistol and fired. The heavy slug tore into the gunman's chest, and he was slammed back against the front wall of Charlotte's house. As he slid down the wall, his eyes open wide in surprise, he left a swath of blood from the exit wound.

Staring up at Jared, Quick's eyes were fast glazing over. "You . . . killed . . . me," he gasped. Then his mouth slackened and his eyes stopped seeing. He was dead.

Charlotte turned away from the sight, clearly shaken by their close call. Putting his arms around her, Jared breathed, "Well, I guess that's that. Case closed."

Looking at him sharply, Charlotte noted, "Then how come your voice doesn't carry the conviction of your words?"

Jared held her at arms' length, searching her face. "Charlotte Baker, I do believe you're getting to know me a little too well," he chuckled. "All right, I confess that I'm a bit stumped by the fifth horseman."

"Who?"

Tugging on his mustache thoughtfully, he stared off into the distance, trying to conjure up an image. "Remember that I told you there were hoofprints of five horses at one of the robbery sites? Well, we've accounted for four of the robbers."

"But you feel there's a person who's still to be added to the tally." Charlotte's words were more a statement than a question.

The Faraday man shrugged. "Well, I suppose that the fifth rider might have had nothing to do with the robberies. Just someone passing through who, coincidentally, stopped at the same spot."

Charlotte peered at him, asking suspiciously, "Do you really believe that?"

He put his hands on her shoulders, gazing intently into her eyes. "I'd sure like to. It'd make my life a whole lot easier."

"What'd make your life easier?" a gruff voice suddenly asked.

Startled, the agent whirled around, then declared, "Josh!"

Pushing back his hat and scratching his forehead with his thumb, the marshal gestured at Tim Quick's body and inquired, "Is this your handiwork, Macalester?"

Jared glanced at Quick, who was still in the same position. The agent noted to himself that it almost looked as if the gunslinger were just sitting there, observing what was going on. Closer examination, however, left no doubt as to his condition.

Turning back to the lawman, Jared—with Charlotte's assistance—filled him in on all that had happened. When they had finished, Josh Wade observed, "You know, I figured it was this son of a bitch all along." He struck a match on the doorframe, lighting the cigarette he had rolled while listening to the couple's story. Then he pointed to the satchel at Quick's feet and asked, "The money's in that bag?"

"Yes."

"Do you want me to take charge of it? Or do you need to send a wire to Matthew Faraday to get further instructions?"

Taken aback that Josh, too, knew of his identity, the agent stared at the lawman.

"Ah, you didn't realize I knew you were a Faraday agent, did you?" the marshal laughed.

"No, I didn't."

"How did you find out?" Charlotte asked.

"Well, simple," Josh explained. "You told Billy, and Billy told me."

The redhead blushed with embarrassment, looking away from Jared's piercing gaze. "Jared, please don't be angry," she begged, "but I did tell Billy who you were."

"Why?"

Josh Wade laughed again, and put his hand on Jared's shoulder. "She was worried about you, my friend. She just wanted Billy to look out for you, that's all. Now, you can hardly blame her for that, can you?"

Sighing, Jared agreed, "I guess not."

"Not that you needed lookin' out for. Anyone who could do what you did—shoot down someone as fast as Tim Quick while he had the drop on you. . . . Well, it seems to me like you can damn well take care of yourself."

After the body was taken away and Josh Wade had left to take care of his usual business, Charlotte invited Jared in for the breakfast she had promised him. Deciding the telegram he needed to send to Matthew Faraday informing him that the case was closed could be better composed on a full stomach, Jared followed Charlotte inside. As they passed the parlor, he happened to glance into the room and noticed a large bundle of newspapers stacked up beside her desk.

"What's all that?" he asked. "Did Johnny forget to deliver the papers while you were gone?"

Charlotte was a few steps ahead of him, but she

stopped and turned around, walking back to see what he was talking about. Looking at the bundle, she smiled and shook her head. "Oh, no, those are the newspapers that are ready for the morgue," she explained. "I had asked Johnny to bring them over while I was gone."

"The morgue? This town doesn't have a morgue. And even if it did, what would they want newspapers for?"

Charlotte laughed. "Not that kind of morgue, the newspaper morgue—which in this case is my attic. All newspapers keep at least one copy of everything they've ever printed. These are copies of the issues printed last month. I'll be putting them into storage with all the others." She smiled sheepishly. "I suppose I like to think that historians might find them interesting a hundred years from now." Patting his shoulder, she told him, "Look through them if you wish while I make us some breakfast."

"Okay, thanks," he responded, walking toward the bundle while Charlotte headed for the kitchen.

Jared casually glanced through the newspapers, reading some articles from issues prior to his arrival in Ironsprings. He then began putting them back into chronological order, but when he saw the issue dated June third, he stopped, puzzling over it. "This doesn't make any sense," he muttered. Grabbing the issue, he hurried to the kitchen.

Holding the newspaper out to Charlotte, he declared, "This isn't the right paper for June third."

"What do you mean, it isn't the right paper?" Charlotte retorted, amused. "Sure it is. Don't you see the date?"

Slightly exasperated, he remarked, "Charlotte, remember I told you I found the paper for June third at the site of the robbery?"

"Yes."

He jabbed the paper with his forefinger. "Well, I read every word of it—every single word—hoping I would get a clue. There was a story about a recent shipment of stoves from St. Louis. I remember it specifically, because my brother is a metalsmith in the very shop that manufactured the stoves."

"Oh, I had to pull that story out," Charlotte told him. "It seems a store in Laramie received the shipment that was supposed to come here."

"What do you mean you pulled the story out? I read it."

Shrugging, she explained, "Well, I mean I had the story set in type, but when I learned that the stoves didn't arrive, I reset the story."

"After you printed a few papers?"

She looked at him quizzically. "No, I didn't print any."

"Then how do you explain the paper I have in my room?"

"I don't know, unless . . ." Charlotte stopped in midsentence. "You know, there is something I remember, but I didn't pay much attention to it at the time. When I realized I had to pull the story, I went back to the office and found that the type had been inked. I don't know why he did it, but Johnny must've printed a paper from that original plate."

"Didn't he mention it?"

"No. In fact, when I came back, Johnny was gone. As I recall, he took off early that day."

"What time was that?"

"I'm not sure. Sometime before ten A.M. I suppose."

The Faraday man walked to the window and stared out, making some quick calculations. As much to himself as to Charlotte he mused, "Allowing enough time for Johnny to have made it to the site of the robbery."

"Jared, you can't be serious!"

He turned and looked at the redhead. "Oh, I'm perfectly serious," he assured her. "Where is he now?"

"I'm not sure. He has a room behind the general store. I imagine he's there."

"I'd better go after him," Jared announced, striding for the doorway. "As soon as word spreads that Quick and the others are dead, Johnny will run. I've got to stop him before he gets away."

Crossing the hallway to the front door, the agent pulled it open just as two shots rang out from nearby.

Startled, Charlotte called, "What was that?"

"I don't know, but I'm about to find out," he replied, darting out the door on the run, his gun in his hand. He raced in the direction of the shots, skidding to a dusty halt in the alley beside the general store. There, standing with a smoking gun in his hand, was Marshal Josh Wade.

"Josh, what happened?" Jared asked as he approached the lawman.

"It's all right, Jared," Josh called. "I got him." The marshal gestured at the man lying face down with a pistol in his hand. It was Johnny Rogers.

"He's the last of the bunch," Josh proclaimed.

"How did you know? I just figured it out myself."

Snickering, Josh put his revolver away and explained, "Actually, it was Billy who figured it out. I should have listened to him in the first place." He stepped to an open doorway at the back of the building and invited, "Come in here. I want to show you something."

Jared followed Josh into the cramped room that had served as Johnny's apartment. Hanging from a hook on the wall was a black leather vest studded with silver conchos—one of which was missing. The conchos were identical to the one Jared had found.

"Billy remembered loaning the vest to Charlotte," the lawman told the agent. "Charlotte gave the vest to Johnny to bring back, but Johnny asked my brother if he could keep it for a while. Billy forgot all about it till you mentioned findin' the concho. Then, when he found out that Johnny was seen by Adam in Sweetwater, playin' poker, he put it all together and arrested him."

Jared Macalester's mouth fell open, and then he asked, "Billy arrested Johnny? When?"

"Yesterday, only I made him turn Johnny loose for

lack of evidence," Josh confessed ruefully. "Then, this mornin', I happened to recall seein' Johnny and Tim Quick talkin' real confidential together in the Pleasure Palace the other night. Whenever anyone came near, they'd shut up. Since we knew that Quick was one of the robbers, I thought I'd come over here and ask Johnny about it. Johnny started actin' pretty suspicious, so I decided to take him over to the jail and hold him for you to talk to. I guess he must've grabbed a gun just before we left his room, 'cause when we came outside and I started walkin' him to my office, he suddenly pulled the pistol out of his pocket. I didn't have any choice, Jared. I had to shoot him."

The Faraday man shrugged and said, "Well, I can't blame you. I just wish I'd gotten a chance to question him, if only to satisfy myself beyond a shadow of a doubt that he was the one."

"How about this?" Josh asked, pulling a loose board away from the wall. "Will this satisfy you?" He reached down inside and took out cash bundled in a paper wrapper printed with the words, "Rocky Mountain Trust."

Nodding slowly, Jared replied, "I guess so." He turned and walked out the door, finding that a number of onlookers had gathered around, including Charlotte Baker.

"No wonder the son of a gun always had money," someone in the crowd mumbled.

"Here comes Prufrock," another man announced as the tall, thin, black-garbed undertaker came solemnly through the crowd.

"I was just attending to Mr. Quick," Prufrock intoned. "I had no idea there would be another to take care of besides."

Stepping out the door, Josh Wade remarked, "Yeah, well, hopefully this one'll be the last."

Jared stood in front of Charlotte, whose face reflected her surprise and regret. Putting a comforting hand on her shoulder, the agent said softly, "I'm sorry about Johnny. I know this is a hard blow for you—not just in terms of your newspaper, but because you really cared about him."

She turned away from the building, and the couple started back toward her house. "I'm just grateful that I have you with me," she told him, her voice breaking slightly. Giving him a sidelong glance, she added in words almost too quiet to be audible, "At least for now."

When they reached her house, Jared sighed and said, "I'll send that wire to Matthew Faraday right after breakfast."

Looking up at him, she remarked, "I guess that Johnny solves the mystery of the fifth horseman."

"Yes, I guess so," Jared agreed. "Now I feel the case is really wrapped up."

They went inside and made their way to the kitchen, and Jared sat down at the table while Charlotte began fixing their breakfast. In the middle of scrambling some eggs, she stopped and shook her head, a look of disquiet on her face.

"What is it?" he asked.

"It's just so odd," Charlotte breathed. "Johnny seldom told me anything about his private life, but I would have never dreamed that he could be the one behind the train holdups."

"Why not?"

"I wouldn't have thought him ambitious enough—or determined enough—to pull off such a thing." She shook her head again. "I guess it's very true what they say: You can't judge a book by its cover."

When George and Charley Stockard, Bates, and Dingus came to town that evening, they found Ironsprings in the midst of boisterous revelry, its citizens using the solving of the railroad robberies as a convenient excuse for a celebration. The four men took a couple of rooms for the night at the Cattlemen's Hotel, but they could have gotten by with only one room, for while George and Dingus went to bed shortly after midnight, Charley and Bates decided to make a long, sodden night of it.

Going from the Bitter Drink to the Bucket of Blood and back again, they got drunker and drunker. And the drunker they got, the more obnoxious they became, until by three in the morning they were picking fights with nearly everyone they encountered. Finally the bartender at the Bitter Drink refused to serve them any more drinks. Furious, Bates drew his gun and began shooting up the place, sending the patrons scattering for cover or running, panicked, out into the street.

Backing out of the saloon, the two men were laughing over their antics when they suddenly crumbled to the ground. Billy Wade had been standing on one side of the door and Josh Wade on the other, and—waiting for just the right moment—the two lawmen brought the butts of their pistols down, knocking both men out.

Calling to a group of four men inside the barroom, Josh ordered, "You fellas, help us get these two down to the jail. They're going to spend the night in the cell."

One of the four men grunted, "If you ask me, that's the best place for 'em. Permanently."

When George and Dingus returned to the Rocking S ranch the next morning, George stormed into the ranch house and confronted Ike Stockard with the news that their brother had been jailed. "I figure we oughta go to town and spring Charley. And I also figure it's about time we settle things with Wade—once and for all," George barked.

"Oh, that's what you figure, is it?" Ike asked, strapping on his gun.

"Well, yeah. I mean, since Josh killed the guy that's been robbin' the trains and all, he's goddamn king of the roost. If we don't take care of him now, there ain't gonna be no livin' with him in that town."

Ike held his hand up, warning, "You stay put out here on this ranch and let me handle this. Charley is hotheaded enough. I don't need to be worryin' about both of you."

Whipping off his hat and throwing it down angrily, George blurted, "Damn it, Ike—"

"Shut up, George! I'm head of this family, and what I say goes." Without another word, he turned on his heels and left the house.

Crossing the yard to the corral for his horse, Ike was waylayed by Dingus, who offered to go to town with him. But Ike refused. "I don't want no trouble, Dingus—and the best way to avoid trouble is for me to go alone."

"There ain't no charge," Josh Wade announced when Ike Stockard arrived at the jail for his brother. Waving his hand toward Billy as a signal to let Charley and Bates out, the marshal continued, "See, your brother Charley and your man Bates shot up the saloon. It was either put 'em in jail or shoot it out with 'em."

Ike sighed. "You did the right thing, Wade," he admitted. "I thank you."

Josh looked at Ike with an expression of surprise on his face. "Well, I'm glad you feel that way, Stockard. By the way, their horses are over at the livery. I suggest you take 'em on home before they find some other trouble to get into."

"That's exactly what I'm gonna do," Ike promised.

"Oh, yeah?" Charley Stockard suddenly put in, entering the office area. He stood bleary-eyed with his hat in his hands for a moment, then, stepping beside his brother, he growled, "I'm hungry. I ain't goin' anywhere till I eat some breakfast."

"All right," Ike agreed reluctantly. "You can eat, but then we go."

The three men left the marshal's office with Ike Stockard shepherding his brother and ranch hand to the restaurant in the Cattlemen's Hotel. Charley and Bates placed their order, and within a few minutes the waitress brought two plates of eggs, potatoes, and fried ham, setting them before the two hung-over men.

Charley Stockard stared blankly at the food for a while, as if having difficulty making his eyes focus. Then he smiled and drawled, "Oh, yeah. I was sittin' here waitin' on a drink, but we must've ordered breakfast." He looked at Ike. "You want some?"

"I ate at home."

Charley pushed his plate aside, then glanced at Bates. The ranch hand, too, was staring at his plate without eating. "That's what I want to do," Charley suddenly proclaimed. "I want to eat at home."

"You should've said somethin' before we ordered breakfast," Ike snapped. "You just spent fifteen cents apiece."

"I don't want the goddamn food!" Charley shouted, shoving his plate off the table onto the floor.

Ike pushed his chair back hard and it scraped noisily on the floor. "I should've let you stay in jail until you sobered up!" he grated, standing up. "Come on, let's go home."

Grabbing the backs of both his charges' collars, the rancher hauled them out of their chairs and guided them out of the restaurant. They stepped into the dusty street, heading for the livery, when Charley abruptly stopped. He was silent for a moment before turning to his brother, asking sharply, "Ike, are we gonna stand up to the Wades?"

"Leave it be, Charley. We got more important things to do than to worry about the Wades."

"There ain't nothin' more important than standin' up like a man," Charley declared. "Now, what about it? If I get braced by the Wades, are you gonna be with me?"

"We don't have any quarrel with the Wades anymore," Ike reminded him. "The cattle's gone, and it'll be a year before we ship any more of 'em. We got no bones to pick with Josh Wade—and we sure as hell ain't mad at Billy."

It was as if Ike had not even spoken, for Charley grinned at the ranch hand and clapped him on the shoulder. "My old buddy Bates'll be with me, won't you, Bates?"

Bates nodded solemnly. "You can count on me."

"What about you, Ike?"

"Let it be," Ike insisted. "We're goin' home."

Shaking his head, Charley held up a finger. "Wait. We ain't goin' home 'till I pick up my boots."

"Your boots?"

"Yeah. I had a new pair made and I aim to pick 'em up," Charley explained as though he were speaking to a not terribly bright young child.

Ike sighed. "All right. We'll go get your boots—but then we're goin' home."

The three men turned to go back to the bootmaker's shop and saw that Josh Wade was watching them.

Standing with his hands on his hips, the marshal blared, "I thought you was takin' 'em home, Ike."

"I am."

"Then get on with it."

"To hell with it!" Charley suddenly shouted, shaking out of his brother's grasp. "To hell with it! Goddamnit, Ike, we ain't gonna be run outta town! I'm callin' you out, Wade. I'm callin' you and your bastard brother out!"

Josh Wade slowly smiled. "All right, have it your way."

Throwing up his hands in disgust, Ike hissed, "Charley, you fool! Now you've done it!"

"You don't have to hang around," Charley said. "There's just two of 'em, so me and Bates'll handle this ourselves."

Ike sighed and loosened the gun in his belt. "Bates isn't a Stockard—so this isn't his fight."

News of the impending showdown spread through the little community like wildfire. Charlotte Baker was just leaving the leather goods store when someone ran along the sidewalk shouting the news at the top of his voice.

"It's a'comin'! The Wades and the Stockards, they're about to shoot it out!"

Staring after the man in disbelief, Charlotte wondered what had happened. She thought everything had been smoothed over and was going well. "Maybe it's a mistake," she muttered aloud. "Maybe it isn't really going to happen."

She stepped to the edge of the boardwalk and looked down the street, and at the sight of scores of people gathering to watch, she knew there was no mistake.

Her first thought was to what effect the gunplay would have on Ironsprings' incorporation. Surely the legislature would not be interested in legalizing a town whose citizens were such savages that they settled their disagreements by shooting each other.

Jared! her mind shouted. *Maybe Jared can stop this!* Charlotte knew he was out at Owen Willoughby's farm, looking over a horse to buy.

She looked frantically around for someone who could go after the Faraday man. Then an acquaintance of hers drove up, reining in across the street, and as the woman started down from her buckboard, Charlotte ran to her, calling, "Mrs. Noble! Please, you must let me borrow your wagon! It's an emergency!"

"Why, yes, of course, dear," Teresa Noble replied, handing over the reins.

Charlotte thanked her, then jumped onto the buckboard. "Giddup!" she shouted, and slapping the reins against the backs of the horses, she had the team in a full gallop by the time they reached the end of the block.

A half-mile from town, Jared had just put a saddle on a big, black stallion and was looking at the horse's conformation. He ran his hand admiringly over the animal's flank, patting it reassuringly.

"Well, what about it, Mr. Macalester?" Owen Willoughby called from his back porch. "You want that horse?"

"He is a good-looking animal," Jared agreed. "But you're asking an awful lot for him."

Willoughby chuckled. "After you've had him a couple of days, you won't think I'm askin' too much," he said with assurance. "Take him and try him out." He then turned toward the house, sniffing the air. Smiling, he announced, "I'd say the coffee's ready. Have a cup."

Giving the stallion one last pat, Jared walked toward the house. "Don't mind if I do."

Willoughby ushered his visitor inside and pointed to a chair. "Have a seat." The farmer poured each of them a cup of the rich brew, handing one to Jared. The Faraday man took a sip and immediately pulled the cup away, looking at it oddly. Willoughby laughed, then asked, "Taste the orange peel, do you?"

"Yes, I do," Jared answered, surprised at the addition.

"I learned that from Josh Wade," Willoughby told him.

Jared Macalester's eyes widened. "Josh Wade!" he echoed. "So—"

Before he got any further, a buckboard came racing into Willoughby's yard. The two men leapt to their feet and hurried to the door just as Charlotte Baker reined in the two frothing horses.

"What is it?" Jared asked as he dashed off the back porch. "What's wrong?"

"Jared, it's the Wades and the Stockards!" Charlotte yelled, panting for breath. "They're about to—"

"I'll take the horse, Mr. Willoughby!" Jared abruptly shouted over his shoulder as he dashed for the horse, knowing what Charlotte was about to say before she had even finished. Leaping into the saddle, he slapped his legs against the animal's flanks and sped out of the yard toward town.

"Get out of the way! Get out of the way!" Jared Macalester shouted as he galloped down Front Street. The people who had gathered for the gunfight immediately opened a corridor to let him through. Reaching the five adversaries, Jared jerked back on the reins so hard that the stallion slid down to its haunches. The agent jumped off the horse and confronted the foes, who stood facing each other in the middle of the street, three men on one side and two on the other.

"What are you doing?" Jared yelled at them. "This is crazy Billy. Why are you—"

"Stay out of this, Macalester," Josh Wade warned, glancing toward him. "This isn't your fight."

"Yeah," Charley agreed, "we ain't never gonna have any peace till this is done."

"The only peace you're going to find is eternal peace!" Jared scoffed.

Charley spat into the dust. "That's better'n no peace at all."

"Ike, what about you?" the agent appealed. "You've got more sense than this."

His face filled with resignation, Ike muttered, "I got no choice, since I reckon this has come down to a family matter. But Bates can pull out if he wants to."

Charley's right hand played nervously just above his gun. "Don't you worry about Bates," he assured his brother. "He's with us, ain't you, Bates?"

"No," Bates suddenly shouted, holding his hands out in front of him. "No, I ain't a part of this. I don't want no part of it."

"Bates, you yellowbelly!" Charley blurted contemptuously. Eyeing the ranch hand, he warned, "Bates, don't be on the ranch when we get back. If you are, I'll kill you."

"You got no right to talk to me like that, Charley Stockard," Bates whined. "You got no right. Not after I took care of Adam like I done."

Ike's head whipped around. "What?" he barked, staring at Bates. "You killed Adam Wade?"

"He had it comin'!" Bates shouted. "Once I was winnin' a poker game over at the Bitter Drink, and one of the guys I was playin' with accused me of cheatin'."

Charley Stockard shook his head incredulously. "What the hell makes that a reason to kill a man?"

"Well, damn it, Charley, when Adam came to break up the fight, he believed the other guy's story, not mine! I hated him for that—hated him real bad. Then when all this stuff started over the cattle, I figured he deserved to be punished. Hell, him and his brothers ain't nothin' but thieves anyway, taxin' the ranchers the way they do—and everybody knows it!"

Staring at his ranch hand, Charley screamed, "That don't give nobody the right to kill a man in cold blood!"

The ranch hand unexpectedly ran for a horse tied to a nearby hitch rail. "Bates!" Josh roared as the man reached the animal, but he was ignored.

Before anyone realized what Bates was doing, he grabbed the shotgun he had spotted holstered on the saddle, then turned and fired, the blast spreading out so wide that the pellets took Charley Stockard and Billy Wade down. A split second later, Josh drew and fired, hitting Bates in the chest. Blood spewed from the front of the ranch hand's shirt, and he was thrown backwards, falling against the frightened horse, which immediately danced out of the way. Despite his wound he tried to raise the shotgun for one more blast, but a second bullet from the marshal's gun knocked him down. This time he lay very still.

"All right, Ike," Josh growled, turning to the rancher, who had not yet drawn his gun, "it's you and me now."

"No!" a woman's voice screamed from up the street. Seconds later, Charlotte Baker boldly guided the buckboard between the two men. Leaping off the seat, she raced to Billy Wade's side and examined his wounds. "Josh, you've got to get these men to a doctor. My God, Billy's your own brother!"

"Later," Josh retorted coldly. "Ike and me'll get our business settled first."

Suddenly Jared Macalester stepped in front of the

marshal and stared at him for a long moment before speaking. "No. You and me'll get our business settled first."

"I can fight my own battles, Macalester," Ike spoke up nervously.

Glancing at the rancher, Jared told him, "My business has nothing to do with you, Stockard. Besides, is this really a battle you want to fight? This town is about to be incorporated. When that happens, you'll have a fair shake. You want to risk it all now?"

Ike lowered his eyes and shook his head. "I . . . I guess not." He looked at Billy and Charley, both sitting up now and being attended to by some of the townspeople. "Are they dying?" he asked.

"No," someone replied. "They just need some buckshot picked out of 'em, is all."

Holstering his gun, Ike sighed and headed toward his brother. "Then come on, Charley. Let's go home."

"Ike, don't come into this town again," Josh railed. "This town is closed to you from now on."

Jared Macalester took a step closer to the marshal. "Josh, you aren't in a position to close this town. The governor has granted me temporary appointment as a territorial marshal—and under that authority, I'm arresting you for train robbery and murder."

There was a collective gasp from the crowd.

"What?" Josh roared. Then he laughed, "Have you gone crazy, Macalester?"

"Nope. *You* were the brains behind all the robberies . . . not Johnny Rogers. You thought that by killing him you'd throw me off, but it didn't work. You see, Johnny left a letter to be opened in case anything happened to him."

Josh Wade's face blackened with rage. "That conniving, blackmailing bastard!" he shouted. Suddenly he reached out and grabbed Charlotte Baker. A couple of the women in the crowd screamed, and some of the men shouted out angrily, but Jared held out a calming hand.

"Be careful, Josh. Don't you hurt her," the agent warned.

Billy Wade lifted himself painfully to his feet, his eyes wide with shock. In a disbelieving voice, he asked, "Josh? Josh, is Jared telling the truth? You're the one?"

"I told you, little brother," the marshal growled, tightening his grip on Charlotte, "being a lawman's an opportunity, not a job. When I saw the opportunity, I grabbed it."

Billy stared at his older brother, a resolute expression on his face. "Josh, if you get away, I'll hunt you down personally."

"You damn fool. It'll be a month before you can even ride again," Josh snorted.

Jared took a small step closer to the lawman. "Tell me, Josh," he asked easily, "how'd you find out about the money shipments?"

Josh snorted again. "That was easy. I just read the messages comin' over the telegraph wire." He smiled and said proudly, "My knowin' how to read Morse code was just one of my secrets."

Jared's hand moved imperceptibly toward his gun. "Yes, well, I guess you weren't quite as smart as you thought you were though, were you?" the agent reminded him.

The lawman's face darkened again. "It was that newspaper . . . that damned paper you found." He shook his head as if doubting he could have made such a glaring mistake. "See, I thought maybe—like had happened once before—the train was gonna be delayed by somethin', meanin' I was gonna have a long wait. I wanted something to read, just in case, so I stopped by the newspaper office to pick up a copy of the *Vindicator*. Johnny'd just set the plates, and he ran me off a copy. I had no idea that Charlotte showed up right after that and changed one of the stories, makin' my copy the only one like it that was printed. But when Johnny learned that you'd found it out at the robbery site, he knew I was the only person who could've left it—and he made me pay for it. He was blackmailing me."

"I'm surprised you let him get away with it for as long as you did."

Josh smirked. "Yeah, well, I figured he might come in handy. I knew he had been wearin' that old vest of Billy's, so I decided to buy myself a little insurance. I took one of the conchos out to the robbery site and left it there, hopin' someone'd find it and implicate Johnny. Then, when you killed Quick, I saw the chance to get rid of the blackmailer—and get myself off the hook at the same time. But I didn't know about the letter." He laughed a short, bitter laugh. "The stupid jerk. If he wrote the letter to protect himself, he should've told me about it. For him to say nothin' about it makes no sense at all."

Jared stared at him silently, then he admitted, "There was no letter, Josh. I just told you that to see what you'd say."

"What? But—? How—? I mean, why'd you even suspect me?"

The Faraday man took a small step closer. "The newspaper wasn't the only clue you left behind. You also left a piece of orange peel in the coffee grounds. I just found out today that you put orange peel in your coffee."

Taking advantage of Josh Wade's diverted attention, Charlotte managed to twist out of his grasp. No longer having a shield to protect him, the marshal brought his gun to bear on Jared, but the agent shot first. The bullet caught Josh high in the chest and he went down, his gun slipping unfired from his fingers.

Jared ran to Josh's side and knelt beside him. Suddenly the dying man opened his eyes, then laughed. "Orange peel?" he asked, his voice weak. "You knew it was me because of the orange peel? That's really funny." He laughed again, but his laughter turned into gasps. Then, with a final rattle in his throat, he died.

Getting to his feet, Jared turned to Charlotte and shook his head, bewildered. "I don't get it. Why was he laughing about the orange peel?"

"I guess it was the irony of it," Charlotte sighed. She looked up at Jared and explained, "You see, about six months ago a man came through town representing the orange growers of California. He set up a booth over in the lobby of the hotel and gave away all sorts of recipes using oranges so more people would buy them. The one that seemed to catch on with just about everybody was putting a piece of orange peeling in a pot of coffee. I'd guess there are probably fifty people in this town who do that now—so the piece of orange peel you found out there could have been left by any one of those fifty."

Putting his arm around Charlotte, Jared stared at Josh Wade's body. "I'll be damned," he breathed. "I'll be damned."

Epilogue

FROM THE *Ironsprings Vindicator,* July 27, 1884:

IRONSPRINGS INCORPORATED!
MARSHAL ELECTED!
VOTE TO TAKE PLACE SOON TO ELECT MAYOR AND CITY COUNCIL!

Ironsprings, Wyoming, has entered into a new era—one we believe will be most prosperous. By the actions of its citizens, first in signing the petition and then voting upon incorporation, our town has shown that it is ready to move into the future.

The initial order of business was to elect a new marshal, and it came as no surprise to this newspaper that our citizens exhibited good sense and judgment in selecting for that important post a man of experience, integrity, and industriousness. We heartily approve of the election of Billy Wade as our first true peace officer.

In one week's time, we will be electing a city council and mayor. Though this newspaper shall make no effort toward influencing the choice of candidates in this first full exercise of our franchise, it shall, in all future elections, take a brave and unabashed stand in endorsing candidates we feel have earned our support.

FARADAY SECURITIES TO OPEN BRANCH OFFICE IN IRONSPRINGS

This newspaper takes great pleasure in welcoming as a new business enterprise an office of the Faraday Security Agency. The Ironsprings office will be staffed by Mr. Jared Macalester, a person known not only to this newspaper but to its readership, and a man respected by all.

Watch for

TRAIN OF GLORY

*next in the Faraday series
coming soon from
Lynx Books!*